MW00625885

THE KINGDOM OF NERETH
TJ Amberson

THE KINGDOM OF NERETH
by TJ Amberson
www.tjamberson.com

ISBN 978-0-9892999-3-0

For my family, who made this possible and did not even know it.

1

The morning sun was just beginning to appear over the Fierlen Mountains as Edlyn made her way toward the stable. In each arm she carried a wooden bucket that had been filled with water from the well. The frigid water splashed rhythmically onto the sides of her dirt-covered dress as she walked, but Edlyn paid the cold no attention. After six years of labor on the manor, she had grown used to her duties. Only once Edlyn reached the stable did she finally set down the heavy buckets to swing open the door.

Inside the stable, the familiar smells of horses and hay drifted through the air. Lifting the buckets again, Edlyn approached the drinking trough and poured in the water, the sound causing the sleeping animals to stir. When the buckets were emptied, Edlyn took a moment to stroke a small gray horse that had poked his head out of a stall to greet her.

"Do not worry, Cynric," she said, smiling. "Breakfast is coming."

After giving the horse another pat, Edlyn picked up a pitchfork and turned to the large pile of hay behind her. She sighed at the unwelcome sight of hay strewn messily about the stable floor. Something had disturbed the pile overnight, and as Edlyn knew, most likely that something was still nestled within.

"Rodents," she muttered with annoyance.

Using the pitchfork, Edlyn made a swift, skillful jab into the hay pile. But it was not the squeal of a creature that she heard in response. Instead, the startled cry of a human reached her ears.

"Get away from here, thief!" Edlyn shouted, and with new fervor she continued stabbing blindly into the hay. "I will not allow you to steal our horses!"

There was another muffled yelp of pain before a young man burst out of his hiding place, dagger in hand. Edlyn gasped, stumbled backward, and raised the pitchfork warningly, prepared to strike again. Covered with hay, the young man stopped when his dark eyes fell upon her. He slowly lowered his arm.

Breathing fast, Edlyn stared silently at the stranger. She decided that he could not be much older than herself—perhaps eighteen or nineteen. He was tall, and his strong features and square jaw led Edlyn to believe that he hailed from another land. The young man's disheveled black hair fell past his ears, and the traces of a beard were on his face. His muddy clothes appeared to be those of a peasant, but their pattern was unfamiliar.

He took a step toward her.

"Get back!" Edlyn cried, lifting her weapon once more.

"Hush," the young man whispered sharply. "I will not hurt you, but you must be quiet."

From his stall, Cynric snorted and restlessly stomped his hooves. Edlyn, however, remained still. Something in the young man's eyes made her believe that he was telling the truth.

"And I am not here to steal your horses," the young man added in an unfamiliar accent, glancing at the pitchfork in Edlyn's hand.

Edlyn followed his gaze and cautiously placed her tool beside Cynric's stall. Keeping her watch on the stranger, she then brushed from her face the long strand of light brown hair that had fallen loose from her braid. The young man observed her without speaking. Somehow, as he noted, her unkempt appearance did not take away from her beauty but rather added to it.

With a shake of her head, Edlyn began wiping her hands on her apron. A glimmer of amusement appeared in her large blue eyes. "You chose an odd place to spend the night, sir."

"Maddock," he said, tracking her. "My name is Maddock."

"Well, Maddock," she went on, rolling up her sleeves, "I have much work to do before Lord Faddin awakes, and thanks to you, I am already behind." She bent down and scooped up some hay. "As it is now morning and you have had your rest, I assume that you shall be on your way."

Without waiting for his response, Edlyn moved to pass but halted abruptly when she saw blood on the ground. Her eyes quickly followed the trail of dark red drops back to Maddock's feet. Raising her head with alarm, she noticed the blood-stained tear in Maddock's dirty shirt.

"You are hurt, sir."

Covering his abdomen with one hand, Maddock took a step toward the stable door. "I will leave. I..."

Maddock trailed off when the chickens outside suddenly began clucking loudly. Edlyn jumped at the unexpected clamor, over which she heard the sound of horses approaching fast. After another glance at the young man, Edlyn rushed by him, opened the stable door, and looked out. Six men on horseback were galloping across the meadow toward the stable. Five of the riders had swords drawn, and the rider in front held a flag aloft—a flag, Edlyn realized with a shudder, which bore the symbol of the infamous Sheriff Hurst.

Edlyn slowly turned to Maddock. "I presume this is about you."

Maddock did not respond. Wincing, he reached out with one arm to brace himself against the wall while keeping his other hand pressed on his abdomen.

"I could be imprisoned for helping a fugitive, or killed," Edlyn went on frankly, shutting the stable door. "It depends on what you have done."

Maddock found his voice, "I will not put you in danger."

He made another move to leave but swayed and began to fall. Edlyn lunged forward, catching Maddock in her arms. Staggering under the weight of his limp body, she lowered him to the dirt.

"Help me leave. I must get away from here," Maddock begged, attempting to get up.

From the sounds outside, Edlyn knew that the riders were nearly upon them. She also saw that Maddock's breathing was growing shallow and the life in his dark eyes fading. He would not escape those who hunted him. For one moment, Edlyn hesitated, looking between Maddock and the stable door. Then she spoke upward, as if to the sky:

"This young man might be an outlaw, but may the spirits of Ravenshire Forest curse me for eternity if I ever help Sheriff Hurst."

Resolved, Edlyn slung Maddock's arm over her shoulders and tugged him to his feet. His head flopped forward while she dragged him to the far end of the stable. Using her foot, she brushed aside some dirt on the ground, uncovering the edges of a wooden door beneath.

"This was once a place for storing food. I used to hide in here as a child. I do not believe that Lord Faddin even knows it exists," she uttered in Maddock's ear, although she was no longer sure that he could hear her.

Edlyn again assisted Maddock to the ground. Hastily kneeling beside him, she gripped the edge of the door and pried it up, exposing a shallow room that had been carved into the earth below. With the noise of the approaching riders pulsating in her ears, Edlyn grabbed Maddock and half-rolled, half-dropped him into the room. As Edlyn slammed the door back into place, the horses came to a stop outside the stable. Leaping to her feet, Edlyn darted to the hay pile and picked up the pitchfork. A second later, the stable door was thrown open.

Edlyn blinked, shielding her eyes from the sunlight. She could see the five armed men still sitting atop their horses. The sixth man, whom she recognized as the sheriff's red-haired deputy, had secured the flag and dismounted from his horse.

"You, girl!" the deputy barked. "We are hunting a young man who is wanted by the king!"

With barely a look at him, Edlyn began loading hay into the feeding trough. "Unless the wanted man is a horse or a chicken, you are searching the wrong place."

The deputy's face twisted angrily. He stormed into the stable. "Are you, servant girl, being disrespectful to me?"

Edlyn raised an eyebrow. "Servant? And who are you, sir? You work for the king, which makes you no more than a servant yourself."

The deputy struck her. There was laughter from the other men as Edlyn stumbled.

"Enough!" someone shouted.

The men went silent. The deputy, positioned to hit Edlyn a second time, dropped his arm and stepped back at the command. Edlyn slowly stood up straight, watching with dread as Sheriff Hurst got down from his horse and strolled into the stable.

"Good morning, Edlyn," the sheriff greeted her.

Edlyn did not reply.

The sheriff reached out and touched her aching cheek. "You must forgive my deputy's behavior."

Edlyn instinctively recoiled at his touch, but she did not move from her place. Sheriff Hurst watched her for a long moment before speaking again:

"You have not seen anything—or anyone— unusual around here this morning, Edlyn?"

"No, sir, I have only seen chickens and horses." She deliberately glanced at the other men. "And a few pigs."

The sheriff chuckled and stroked his dark mustache. He then turned to his men. "Search the grounds. I will go speak to Lord Faddin."

The deputy and soldiers departed. The stable door closed behind them, leaving Edlyn and the sheriff alone. She put her head down and continued filling the trough, pretending not to notice the way that he studied her movements.

The uncomfortable quiet was broken by a faint sound from the far end of the stable, which was followed by another. Edlyn's heart thudded within her chest. She knew that one moan—one delirious sound from the injured Maddock—would be enough to have them both killed. She uneasily peeked at the sheriff, but he seemed not to have heard the noises. He was still observing her.

"It is a pity that a beautiful young woman should be working in such a place as this," he remarked.

Edlyn was about to answer when she again noticed the blood stains on the ground. She slid forward and stood over them, concealing the evidence of Maddock's presence from the sheriff's view. The sheriff smiled, moved closer to her, and added:

"Edlyn, you do not have to live like this."

The sounds from the back of the stable ceased. Edlyn shifted anxiously. With every passing second, Maddock was growing weaker. She needed to get to him.

The sheriff cleared his throat expectantly.

Distracted, Edlyn faced the unwanted visitor once more. "I will leave here one day, Sheriff Hurst, when I have enough money to buy my freedom."

"Edlyn, you do not have to wait. You know that I am offering you freedom now."

He then came so near that every impulse in Edlyn's body warned her to flee. Yet she stayed still, hiding the drops of Maddock's blood under her feet. A pleased expression appeared on the sheriff's face as he cupped her chin in his hand and went on:

"Comfort, riches, connections with the king— surely you realize what my offer of marriage means for you."

Edlyn reached up and pulled his hand from her face. "Freedom, indeed. I shall be no one's, sir. Especially not yours."

Sheriff Hurst gripped Edlyn's arm and yanked her to him. "You speak as though you have a choice in the matter, but you will do as I desire. I have watched you for far too long, Edlyn. You—"

The sound of the stable door being opened interrupted him. The sheriff released his grip on Edlyn and pushed her away.

"The men have found nothing on the manor grounds, and the serfs do not report anything atypical," the deputy announced. "Lord Faddin is awake and ready to meet with you."

"Very well," Sheriff Hurst replied. He gestured dismissively toward Edlyn. "There is nothing of interest here, either."

The sheriff marched from the stable. With a smirk, the deputy followed. As soon as they were gone, Edlyn rushed to the door and checked outside. The deputy and soldiers were departing, and Sheriff Hurst was riding toward the manor house alone. Wasting no time, Edlyn spun around and ran to the far side the stable.

"Maddock?" she called out as loudly as she dared, heaving the hidden door up.

The faintest of mumbles came in reply. He was still alive.

Edlyn jumped down into the tiny room, wrapped her arms around Maddock's chest, and pulled him to his feet. "I cannot lift you out on my own," she told him. "Have you any strength left?"

Maddock raised an arm and began attempting to boost himself upward. He was weak, but it was enough. Edlyn threw her body against his and hefted him to the floor above. Maddock collapsed from the effort and became still.

"You cannot stop here," Edlyn told him, frightened by his pallor. "There is a room over this stable where no one else goes. Come."

Maddock moaned when Edlyn again hung his arm over her shoulders and pulled him to his feet. Together, they struggled across the stable to a narrow, wobbling staircase behind Cynric's stall and began to climb. The staircase appeared to come to a dead end as it met the ceiling, but Edlyn reached out and pushed a board aside, revealing the opening to a room above.

"Come quickly," Edlyn instructed, assisting Maddock upward.

The attic room that they entered was small, and the air smelled stale. Sunlight filtering in through the broken roof panels revealed a thick layer of undisturbed dust on the floor. There was nothing in the room but a dingy cot in one corner.

"You must rest," Edlyn panted, nearly having to carry Maddock across the floor.

When they reached the cot, Maddock fell upon it. His sunken eyes moved to Edlyn's face. He opened his mouth as if to speak, but his eyes rolled back and closed. With a gasp, Edlyn leaned over him. The sensation of warmth upon her check told her that he was still breathing.

Scrambling to her feet, Edlyn rushed down the staircase and to the front of the stable. Snatching up a bucket, she began scooping water out of the drinking trough, but once again, the sound of an approaching horse forced her to stop. She slid to the stable door and peered out. Sheriff Hurst had left the manor house and was riding by the stable, a satisfied expression on his face. Edlyn ducked back, waiting until the sound of his horse's hooves faded. Then she grabbed the water and sped to the attic.

Maddock was motionless on the cot, and his eyes remained closed. Setting the bucket beside her, Edlyn knelt down and tore open Maddock's blood-soaked shirt. She swallowed hard when she saw the gaping wound in his lower right side—a wound that had surely come from a sword.

"This will hurt," Edlyn warned.

Lifting the bucket high, she turned it over and let the cold water flush over his abdomen. Maddock made a sound and opened his eyes.

"Stay still," Edlyn told him, relieved to see some life in his face. She bent forward and began examining his injury more closely. "It appears that you managed to dodge your attacker's blow just in time, Maddock. I believe that you will live to cause trouble yet."

Edlyn reached around her waist, untied her apron, and pulled it off from over her dress. Working quickly, she wrapped the apron around Maddock's abdomen and cinched it tight. He let out a groan.

"I need more dressings," Edlyn announced, getting to her feet. "I will return soon. I..."

Edlyn's throat suddenly tightened when she saw a symbol burned into the skin of Maddock's left shoulder—a symbol she had seen once before.

"You are from the Colleland," Edlyn barely managed to utter.

Very slowly, Maddock lifted his head. "I am from the Colleland."

Edlyn cringed and moved a step away from him.

Maddock's dark eyes followed her. "You have done enough for me already. I will go."

He tried sitting up but dropped back with a cry. Shaking, Edlyn bent over him, using both hands to keep him from moving.

"No, Maddock, you must rest."

Maddock gripped Edlyn's arm, bracing himself until a wave of pain subsided. Then he spoke, his breathing labored, "Your name...the men who came into the stable...called you Edlyn?"

Edlyn could only stare at the stranger. After six long years, a man from the Colleland was before her once again. It took all her will to keep her voice steady as she eventually answered:

"Yes, my name is Edlyn."

"Thank you, Edlyn."

She stood up. "I will go for supplies. You will be here for several days."

Edlyn left Maddock and flew down the stairs. Bursting out of the stable, she ran for the manor house without looking back.

She was going to save the life of one whom she had sworn to kill.

2

"Edlyn, tell me about the man who questioned you this morning."

Edlyn glanced at Maddock. "I did not realize that you heard our conversation."

"I heard it all."

The quiet fierceness in Maddock's tone caused Edlyn to look at him again. He was watching her closely.

"That man was Sheriff Hurst," Edlyn explained, not hiding her disdain. "He is friends with Lord Faddin. He comes to the manor far too often, I am afraid."

"What else do you know about Sheriff Hurst?"

Edlyn made herself busy soaking cloths in the bowl of healing potion beside her. "Nothing of importance."

"And the one who struck you? Who was he?"

"The sheriff's deputy."

"The deputy is a coward."

"They are all cowards."

There was a pause.

"You cannot mean that you have been struck before."

"Not by the deputy, no."

Maddock's expression changed. It was a long time before he spoke again:

"I also heard them say you are a servant here. Is that true?"

Edlyn did not give him an answer. Instead, she lifted a cloth out of the potion and faced him squarely. "Lie back," she instructed.

Keeping his eyes on hers, Maddock obeyed. Edlyn slid closer and set the saturated cloth on Maddock's injury.

He winced. "It burns."

"So complains the young man who had a sword wound in his side but said nothing about it."

A slight grin appeared on Maddock's face.

"The burning is good," Edlyn added, nearly smiling, too. "It means that this potion is working."

He adjusted his position to see her better. "Why does a young woman who is already doing the work of three men on a manor also know how to make healing potions?"

"My father taught me."

"Where is your father now?"

"Dead," she answered, removing the first cloth and replacing it with another.

"When did he die?"

"Six years ago. I was eleven."

"What about your—"

"My mother died when I was born. My father raised me alone, and he..."

Edlyn could not finish, stopped by an unexpected swell of emotion evoked by thoughts of her childhood. She could still vividly recall the countless happy nights when her father had taught her by candlelight after the other serfs had gone to sleep. Life then had been much more simple and good.

Maddock remained quiet, waiting.

Once Edlyn was sure that her voice would stay steady, she continued to speak, filling the silence, "My father was a serf on this manor. When I was very young, a fire broke out in the manor house. My father saved Lord Faddin's life. In return, Lord Faddin swore that he would care for me should anything ever happen to my father."

Maddock scowled. "Keeping you as an overworked serf seems a poor fulfillment of that promise."

Edlyn blinked hard as she set a new cloth on Maddock's abdomen. "I receive wages for my work, at least. One day, I will have enough money to buy my freedom."

"Freedom is not something you should have to purchase."

"There are many things in the Kingdom of Nereth that are not as they should be, Maddock."

He observed her. Edlyn felt her cheeks grow warm under his pensive gaze, and she averted her eyes.

"How did your father die?" he inquired after a while.

"You ask many questions," Edlyn pointed out. "I have yet to ask any of you."

Maddock rested his head back. "But I believe that you already know much about me."

Edlyn glanced uncomfortably at the symbol on his shoulder. "My father taught me about the Colleland."

"That is an unusual thing for parents to teach their children. Most in Nereth do not believe the tales of the Colleland anymore."

"My father believed. He said that he even met the Man in White."

There was a startled silence before Maddock sat up and searched Edlyn's face.

"What else did your father teach you?"

Edlyn shrugged. "He told me the same stories that everyone knows. That is all."

"Edlyn, I want to hear what you were taught."

The urgent way that Maddock spoke struck Edlyn deeply. Setting the cloths down, she sat back and replied:

"Very well, Maddock. I was taught that, centuries ago, King Whittemoor ruled the Kingdom of Nereth. After King Whittemoor's death, his eldest son, Tiernan, was the rightful heir to the throne. But the king's daughter, a powerful sorceress named Raelin, and his younger son, a warrior named Guthrie, conspired to take control of Nereth for themselves. With promises of wealth and power, Raelin and Guthrie convinced many to support them. Soon, the people of this land were fiercely divided. War broke out. Death spread across the land. Tiernan and his surviving followers had no choice but to go into hiding. Where they fled to is a mystery, but it has always been referred to as the Colleland."

Edlyn stopped, aware of how much she was talking. She was not used to having a man listen to her the way that Maddock was doing. Self-consciously, Edlyn ducked her head and resumed her work.

"Go on," Maddock encouraged.

Edlyn raised her eyes. Maddock's attention remained focused on her, and she found something perplexingly disarming—reassuring—about it. Brushing a strand of hair from her eyes, she continued:

"With the Kingdom of Nereth theirs, Raelin and Guthrie cast aside the promises they had made to those who supported them, and they began a tyrannical reign. Since that time, the evil magic of Raelin and Guthrie has been passed down from one king and queen to the next, keeping those who are devoted to evil on the throne while the people of Nereth suffer. As for Tiernan, many in Nereth believe that he and his followers died of starvation. But my father said that

Tiernan and his people survived, only prevented from returning to Nereth by a curse that Raelin put over this kingdom those many years ago."

"And the Man in White?"

Placing another cloth over Maddock's wound, Edlyn went on, "Despite Raelin's curse, the Man in White was somehow able to come to Nereth from the Colleland. Over the centuries, there have been many sightings of the Man and White throughout the kingdom. The Man in White even came to my father and told him that, one day, a descendent of Tiernan will return to Nereth, reclaim the throne, and unite the kingdom."

When Edlyn finished, she was surprised that Maddock said nothing. Clearing her throat, she bent down and inspected his wound. The tissues were already beginning to heal.

"Edlyn, do you believe what your father taught you?"

She did not look at him. "I used to believe it all, Maddock, but I do not anymore."

"What changed?"

Once again, Edlyn could not speak, this time rendered speechless by terrifying, sickening memories of what she had witnessed on a night long before. With bitter tears pricking her eyes, Edlyn dropped her head and let out a sob.

A firm hand grasped her clenched one.

"Edlyn?"

Edlyn raised her head. Maddock was watching her, eyes wide with concern. Edlyn pulled her quivering arm from his hold.

"I used to believe, Maddock, until the night when I saw my father's murder. He was killed by a man who had the symbol of the Colleland on his left shoulder, just like you."

The color left Maddock's face.

Edlyn stood up and moved for the stairs. "Lord Faddin will be expecting his dinner soon," she told him coolly. "I must be off."

***

Edlyn finished putting new dressings on Maddock's injury. "Your wound was from a sword, Maddock. A skillfully placed wound, at that. Who tried to kill you?"

"Ah, today must be your day to ask the questions," Maddock noted.

"Perhaps."

"And perhaps you wish that my assailant's strike had finished me off?"

Edlyn eyed him. "Had I wished you dead, Maddock, I would have left you to bleed to death when I found you yesterday morning. Even worse, I would have turned you over to Sheriff Hurst."

"You believe that being with Sheriff Hurst is a fate worse than death."

"Yes."

Maddock almost seemed pleased. "Well, since you have not committed me to Sheriff Hurst's hands, then you must not hate me after all, Edlyn."

Edlyn found herself disconcertingly flustered. She quickly threw her head back. "You should not be so hasty to assume."

His expression remained steady. "Neither should you."

Edlyn decided to change her attention to the basket beside her. Reaching inside, she took out a roll, a piece of cheese, and a small jug of fresh milk. She handed everything to Maddock. He consumed the meal ravenously. Once he was done, he settled his concentration on her again.

"It was Sheriff Hurst who dealt me this blow, Edlyn."

Edlyn's mouth dropped in surprise.

"There, I have answered you," Maddock went on, settling back to rest. "However, from the curious look in your blue eyes, I suspect that my answer has only generated more questions. You are free to ask. I will answer what I can."

Edlyn needed no further encouragement. "The deputy said that you were wanted by the king. What did you do to earn such a distinction?"

"I am on an errand that the king and queen do not approve of."

"That I have already deduced, since Sheriff Hurst himself is hunting for you," Edlyn remarked in a tone that did not disguise her annoyance.

Maddock faced her. "Perhaps I now have a reason to be on the hunt for your Sheriff Hurst, too."

"Do not insult me," Edlyn retorted. "He is not *my* sheriff."

"Insult you? I do not mean to insult you. I only state what I know: Sheriff Hurst works for the king, he has wealth and rank, and out of the entire kingdom, he has selected you as the object of his desire. That must be quite an honor."

Edlyn vehemently shook her head. "Object, indeed, for that is all I would be to him. I have no desire to be pursued by such a man. So intentional or not, your words are insulting."

"Then I offer my apologies, although I admit that I am left to wonder: if riches, protection, rank, and comfort cannot entice you to marry, what man could ever have the chance to win your heart?"

Edlyn was irritated to sense that she was blushing. "I do not intend to marry."

"That is an unusual thing to hear a young woman say."

"There are other things that I plan to do with my life."

"But what if you fall in love?"

Edlyn stoical expression faltered. "I thought this was my day to ask the questions."

"I suppose that is only fair," Maddock relented, the corners of his mouth turning up slightly.

Edlyn nodded, content once more. "With Sheriff Hurst on your trail, you are undoubtedly a marked man throughout the kingdom. Your story must be quite intriguing. I want to know what mission you are on, Maddock. "

Maddock pushed his thick hair back. "That is something I cannot tell you."

"Why? Are you afraid that I still might turn you in?" Edlyn haughtily gathered her things and stood to go. "While it may be my day to ask questions, Maddock, it has indeed been yours to make insults."

"No, Edlyn, that is not the reason," he quickly replied, and he seemed to choose his words carefully before going on, "There are just some things that could put you at risk of harm if you knew about them."

Edlyn felt a shiver run through her. "I must be off, Maddock. I will see you in the morning."

***

"You are later than usual this morning, Edlyn. I was beginning to believe that you had grown tired of me at last."

Edlyn made no reply. Wearing a cloak over her dress, she stiffly knelt beside the cot and removed the bandages from Maddock's wound. She was satisfied by what she saw. In only three days, his wound had nearly healed.

"You are pale," Maddock noted, his grin disappearing.

"No, it is only the dim light in here."

Edlyn put on a smile and handed Maddock his breakfast. But the slight tremor of her arm did not go unnoticed by Maddock's sharp eye. He sat up abruptly, slid to the edge of the cot, and took both of her hands in his.

"You are not well. Are you sick?"

"I am not sick."

Maddock did not release her. "Something is wrong."

"I brought you fresh clothing," Edlyn changed the subject, pulling from his grip. "They belonged to a serf who once worked here."

"Where is that serf now?"

"He was sold, like so many others. Lord Faddin's drunken, squandering ways have forced him to sell both things and people in order to pay his taxes. There are not half as many serfs on the manor now as there were when I was young. But even as resources grow ever more scarce, Lord Faddin continues to indulge himself." She shook her head, disgusted. "Were it not for the promise Lord Faddin made to my father, I am sure that I, too, would have been sold."

Edlyn set out the rest of the food and gathered her things. When she stood up to leave, however, she let out a cry of pain and doubled over.

Maddock jumped to his feet. "Edlyn, what is it?"

"It is nothing." Edlyn was not quite steady as she backed up from him. "You are almost healed, Maddock. One more day should be all you need. I must depart but shall see you early tomorrow."

As Edlyn turned to go, Maddock reached out and pulled on the clasp of her cloak. The cloak fell to the floor before Edlyn could stop it, revealing the back of her dress, which was covered with long, blood-stained tears.

"You have been whipped. Who whipped you?" Maddock demanded, breathing hard. "Who whipped you in this way?"

"It does not matter. I—"

"Who did this?"

"Lord Faddin," Edlyn replied without emotion.

Maddock's jaw clenched, but his enraged expression slowly changed to one of agonized realization.

"Edlyn, your regular work on the manor...you have not been able to take care of your usual chores because you have been attending to me, have you?"

"I was late with Lord Faddin's wine this morning, that is all," Edlyn answered, looking anywhere but at him. "It is no matter. Lord Faddin will be drunk and forget soon enough."

Maddock stooped down, picked up the cloak, and gently set it over Edlyn's shoulders. "How long until you will have enough money to be free from this place?"

"A while yet," she told him, pulling the cloak around her.

Brow furrowed, Maddock gestured to the remnants of the food Edlyn had brought him. "Edlyn, whose meal was this?"

"Yours, of course."

"That is not what I meant. With resources on this manor so scant, surely there is not extra food to come by." Maddock fixed his stare upon her. "Whose meal was this supposed to have been? For whom were all the meals intended, before you gave them to me?"

Edlyn went to the stairs. "All the healing potions in the kingdom would have been for nothing, Maddock, if you did not also have the nutrition to recover."

Maddock opened his mouth but could not speak.

"Eat, change, and rest," Edlyn ordered. "I will be back at first light to confirm that you are fully recovered and ready to be on your way."

3

"It seems you are gettin' up earlier and earlier to complete your chores, Miss Edlyn."

Edlyn finished stacking wood near the kitchen stove. "Am I?" she asked the woman who had addressed her, feigning surprise.

"It is not right that you are expected to do so much work around here," the plump woman went on, shaking her head. "Lord Faddin dishonors your father's very name with the way he treats you."

Edlyn moved to the table in the center of the kitchen and sat down. The woman placed a meager breakfast before her.

"I took a little extra from the rations," the woman informed her in a hushed voice. "I want you to eat it all. You are not appearin' well, miss."

Edlyn's empty stomach growled as she eyed the food. She gave a grateful smile to the woman who had been in charge of the serfs' kitchen for as long as she could remember.

"Thank you, Lancy."

"It is nothin'. I only wish I could do more for you, miss." Lancy's eyes glistened before she wiped her hands on her apron and moved back to the stove. "Now eat up. I want to see you regain your health."

Edlyn pulled off a small corner of bread and chewed slowly. Once Lancy's back was turned, Edlyn wrapped the rest of the meal in a cloth and hid it under her apron. She waited a while before standing up.

Lancy looked over at her. "Are you done already, miss? I am happy to see that you have got your appetite back. I was beginnin' to..."

At the sound of an approaching carriage, Lancy broke off from what she was saying, bustled to the window, and peeked outside.

"It is that filthy Sheriff Hurst again," Lancy muttered, turning to scan the kitchen. "No doubt he and Lord Faddin will want somethin' to eat. That will be another meal comin' out of the serfs' rations." She took a hurried step to the stove. "Do not stay to help me, miss. Get yourself away from the sheriff. I will manage on my own."

Edlyn nodded appreciatively. "I shall return as soon as he is gone."

Edlyn pushed open the kitchen door. She stepped out into the crisp morning air but came to an abrupt halt, barely suppressing an exclamation of surprise. The sheriff's deputy was standing in her path, almost as if he had been waiting for her.

"Good morning, Edlyn. It is Edlyn, correct?" the deputy inquired with mock politeness.

Edlyn nodded slightly.

"The sheriff said that I might find you leaving the manor house this way," he chuckled.

A noise caused Edlyn to check over her shoulder. Lancy had come to the doorway. The woman exchanged an uneasy glance with Edlyn, and then she put on a smile and addressed the unwanted visitor:

"Good mornin', sir. I apologize that I did not see you standin' out here. Please come in, and I will get you somethin' to drink."

The deputy sneered. "I do not want a drink. I am here to fetch the girl. Lord Faddin and Sheriff Hurst would like to speak with her."

Instantly, Edlyn was overcome with fear. The deputy's task could only mean that Maddock had been discovered, and that Sheriff Hurst and Lord Faddin were going to interrogate her about him. With a sickening sense of dread, Edlyn's eyes drifted to the stable in the distance as she wondered if Maddock was even still alive.

"Edlyn, surely you realize that you should not keep the men waiting."

Edlyn focused again on the deputy, who was watching her with a patronizing expression on his face. Edlyn stood up straight, keeping her emotions hidden. She would not give him the pleasure of knowing that she was afraid.

"I am ready, sir."

With a last look at Lancy, Edlyn reentered the kitchen. The deputy followed close behind. Stiff and silent, Edlyn walked across the room and stepped through the serfs' door into a narrow passageway. Moving down the corridor with the deputy on her heels, Edlyn's sense of foreboding became almost more than she could bear. She did not want to think about what might have happened to Maddock, yet she was desperate to know the fate of the young man from the Colleland. Only once Edlyn reached the closed door at the end of the passageway did she break from her agonizing thoughts and pause.

"Edlyn, is something wrong?" she heard the deputy inquire, sounding amused.

Edlyn made no reply. Reaching out with an unsteady hand, she pushed the door open, the harsh sound echoing ominously through the passageway. Then, taking a deep breath, Edlyn stepped into Lord Faddin's dining hall.

The room was long and dank, with its floor and walls made from stone. High on the right, a large stained-glass window glowed in the sunlight. A massive chandelier hung over the center of the room by a thick chain, and directly beneath the chandelier was an ornately carved wooden table. As usual, Lord Faddin was seated at the far end of the table by the fireplace, sipping on wine. Sheriff Hurst stood near Lord Faddin, his hand resting upon the hilt of his sword. The two men broke off from their conversation when Edlyn entered. Lord Faddin drunkenly set down his glass and peered at her.

"You wanted to see me, sir?" Edlyn inquired, her shaky voice betraying her.

A scraping sound caused Edlyn to start and check behind her. The deputy had entered the dining hall and shut the door. Edlyn watched as he placed a large beam across the door, locking it from the inside. Her body went cold.

"Edlyn, step closer. I cannot see you in the shadows," Lord Faddin ordered, his speech slurred.

She turned again to her master. Out of the corner of her eye, she saw the deputy walk to the far end of the room and stand beside Sheriff Hurst.

"I said come closer, you pathetic animal," Lord Faddin repeated irritably.

Edlyn took a single step forward.

Lord Faddin seemed satisfied. He crossed his arms over his belly. "Edlyn, I promised your father that I would care for you, did I not?"

Edlyn was taken aback by the question. "Yes, sir, you did."

"Little did I know what a useless burden you would be," Lord Faddin went on sloppily, "but I have kept my promise to your father nonetheless."

The deputy laughed. Beside him, the sheriff observed in silence.

Lord Faddin sighed and motioned around the stark room. "Sadly, every year since I made that promise, it has been harder to find the money that I need to pay my taxes. I have often wondered how I could continue to afford a worthless girl like you." He shook his head, took another long drink, and went on, "But I have just come to a marvelous agreement with Sheriff Hurst—an arrangement that will allow me to fulfill my promise to your father and yet get you off my hands, while also freeing me from the burden of paying taxes."

Edlyn began looking questioningly between the men. It was clear that the conversation had nothing to do with Maddock, after all. But while Edlyn felt relief on Maddock's behalf, a new and unnerving discomfort was rising within her.

"It is a simple solution, really," Lord Faddin rambled on, clearly pleased. "Although a peasant hardly deserves what you are about to receive."

The deputy chortled once more. Sheriff Hurst's expression did not change. Lord Faddin took a last drink of his wine before setting the cup resolutely onto the table.

"Edlyn, I have sold you," he announced.

"Sold me?" she repeated, stunned.

Lord Faddin sat back. "Yes, you stupid thing. I have sold you to Sheriff Hurst. You are his now."

Edlyn reached for a chair to steady herself.

"A perfect solution, really," Lord Faddin went on, ignoring Edlyn's distress. "You will be cared for—although you do not deserve to be—and thus I shall fulfill my promise to your father. In return for giving you to him, Sheriff Hurst has arranged that I will no longer pay taxes."

Edlyn could not speak. She could not move.

"Now, as it is all settled, you are no longer my concern." Lord Faddin unsteadily got up. "You shall be taken away immediately. Farewell."

Gripping the chair more tightly, Edlyn finally found her voice, "No. I will not go."

The sheriff raised an eyebrow and peered over at Lord Faddin.

Lord Faddin's face flushed angrily. "What did you say?"

"I said that I will not go," Edlyn repeated more boldly.

Lord Faddin stumbled to her, the scent of alcohol strong on his breath. Raising his hand, he struck her down to the floor.

"You will do exactly what Sheriff Hurst tells you to do," Lord Faddin seethed. "You are his property now."

The deputy approached and tugged Edlyn to her feet. "You will learn not to be so ungrateful," he spat resentfully. "Have you no respect for the life of privilege that Sheriff Hurst has chosen to provide you?"

Through vision blurred by tears, Edlyn saw Sheriff Hurst coming forward, stroking his dark beard while he inspected her.

"I am sorry that things are off to such a poor start, Edlyn," the sheriff remarked soothingly, using one hand to caress her braided hair. "However, I am sure that, in time, you will learn to appreciate me."

Edlyn tried to yank away, but the deputy shoved her into the sheriff's arms.

"That is better," the sheriff stated, keeping Edlyn close to him. He nodded to the deputy. "Since our little arrangement has been settled, let us make our journey back to the castle."

"No!" Edlyn screamed, struggling to free herself. "No!"

The sheriff clamped his hands around Edlyn's arms and started pulling her toward the door. She could hear the deputy and Lord Faddin laughing as she desperately fought against the sheriff's hold.

Suddenly, there was the loud sound of shattering glass, and sunlight began pouring more brightly into the room as colorful pieces of the broken window rained down to the floor. Lord Faddin shrieked with surprise. The deputy shielded himself under his cape. The sheriff, still holding Edlyn, spun toward the noise and drew his sword. Raising her head, Edlyn let out a cry.

Maddock was standing on the window ledge high above, pieces of stained glass at his feet and his dagger in his hand. Maddock's face was pale and emotionless, but his eyes were furious as he stared down at the sheriff.

"Let her go," Maddock said.

The deputy peeked out from under his cape. "Come down, you coward! Come down!"

"Intruder!" Lord Faddin bellowed at the same time. "How dare you invade my manor? Who are you?"

Maddock kept his eyes on Sheriff Hurst. "I said, let her go."

The sheriff's shocked expression became replaced by a sinister, entertained smile. He raised his sword higher. "Ah, this is a most welcome surprise. Now I shall have two prizes in one day: the girl for me and the outlaw to bring to the castle." The sheriff tipped his head, observing Maddock more closely. "I see that you have healed remarkably well from my last blow, young man. It is no matter, though. I shall take you to the king and queen, and they will have you tortured and killed."

Maddock made a lightning-quick scan of the room. "I am warning you for the last time. Release her."

"A noble effort," Sheriff Hurst remarked with a pitying laugh. "However, as you have undoubtedly noticed, it is three against one. You are recently injured and also outnumbered. You cannot win this fight, and you will not escape. Surrender, or we will kill you immediately."

"Maddock, get out of here before they kill you!" Edlyn screeched. "Go, Maddock!"

The sheriff's confident expression disappeared. He whipped Edlyn around and examined her face, his own becoming blanched and livid as realization seemed to strike him. "What is this, Edlyn? You know this outlaw's name? You care for him?"

"She has surely been providing him aid!" the deputy proclaimed, waving his sword. "She has been helping the enemy! She has disgraced you in every way, Sheriff!"

Lord Faddin also started to holler, "Traitorous girl! You dishonor the sheriff, the king, and the queen! You bring shame upon me! You must die!"

Swaying from intoxication, Lord Faddin unsheathed his sword and prepared to charge for Edlyn, who remained trapped in the sheriff's arms.

"Stay back, Lord Faddin," Sheriff Hurst ordered with disdain, moving Edlyn behind him.

But Lord Faddin lurched forward with his weapon. "No! I will not let her ruin our names!"

As Lord Faddin stumbled closer, Sheriff Hurst flung Edlyn out of his arms. When she hit the floor, Edlyn saw the sheriff raise his own sword to block Lord Faddin's strike.

"Do not stop me, Sheriff Hurst!" Lord Faddin roared as their weapons clashed. "The girl does not deserve to live!"

Sheriff Hurst, the younger and stronger of the two, easily pushed Lord Faddin away. "How dare you speak to me in such a way. This girl is my property. I will do with her as I please."

"But she disgraces us with every breath she takes!" Lord Faddin declared hysterically.

While the two men fought, Edlyn scrambled to her feet and lunged for the door. But a sharp kick in the back of her knees caused her to fall once more.

"Where do you think you are going?" she heard the deputy scornfully inquire.

Edlyn rolled over and flinched. The deputy stood over her, threateningly pointing his sword.

"Stop!" Lord Faddin yelled at the deputy. "I want her death to come by my hand!"

With another drunken cry, Lord Faddin charged again for Edlyn. Edlyn only had time to scream before Sheriff Hurst stepped between them and, with one fast movement, drove his own sword into Lord Faddin's chest.

Lord Faddin made a terrible gurgling noise. Eyes bulging, he turned his face to the sheriff. Sheriff Hurst's expression was like stone as he pulled his sword out of his friend's chest. Lord Faddin dropped to his knees and collapsed.

The room was silent.

"Lord Faddin?" Edlyn whispered, weakly reaching out.

Lord Faddin did not reply. Face down on the cold floor, he was dead in an expanding pool of his own blood.

"Get up, Edlyn," the sheriff snapped, reaching down and bringing her to her feet. "Watch as I do the same thing to the outlaw whom you think that you care so much about."

Holding Edlyn tightly, Sheriff Hurst raised his blood-stained sword and turned to the window ledge.

Maddock was gone.

"Where did he go?" the sheriff demanded.

"He must have leapt out the window." The deputy rushed to open the door. "I will sound the alarm. He cannot have gotten far. We—"

"No," the sheriff interrupted, peering into the dark corners of the room. "I saw the look in his eyes. He would not leave the girl. He is still here. Somewhere."

With a whimper, the deputy left the door closed, refaced the center of the room, and nervously adjusted his grip on his sword.

Keeping his own weapon ready, Sheriff Hurst positioned Edlyn as a shield in front of him. "Come out, boy!" he called, his voice resonating.

Nothing stirred.

Edlyn gasped fearfully when she felt the tip of the sheriff's sword being pressed against her neck.

"Come out or I will slit her throat!" Sheriff Hurst warned.

Edlyn frantically surveyed the room. She saw nothing except the empty table and Lord Faddin's body on the ground.

"He is not here, Sheriff," the deputy insisted. "We are losing time. We must leave now if we hope to follow his trail."

After a moment's deliberation, the sheriff appeared to consent. He sheathed his sword and shoved Edlyn toward the door. But as he took a step to follow, Sheriff Hurst stopped and shook his head.

"No. I am certain he did not leave her."

Sheriff Hurst again grasped Edlyn and jabbed the tip of his sword to her neck. "This is your last chance, boy! She dies if you do not surrender!"

A sound above caused them all to look up. The chandelier overhead was swaying, causing the chain from which it hung to groan. Unnaturally, the chandelier picked up momentum, and as it swung from shadow into sunlight, a figure could be seen crouched upon it.

"Maddock!" Edlyn exclaimed.

Dagger aloft, Maddock leapt from the chandelier and came down on top of the deputy. The deputy kicked furiously, throwing Maddock off of him. Maddock landed hard on the stone, striking his head, and did not move.

"No!" Edlyn cried out, attempting to break away from the sheriff.

"Take the boy's weapon and tie him up," Sheriff Hurst ordered the deputy, keeping Edlyn restrained. "We shall bring him to the king and queen. I want him tortured for his defiance."

The deputy did not answer. Still holding Edlyn in front of him, the sheriff turned to him. Edlyn saw the deputy standing quietly, one hand on his sword and the other pressed against his left ribs. Slowly, the deputy looked down and pulled his hand away from his body. Blood coated his fingers, and there was a dagger wound in his chest. The wound was small, but Edlyn knew it would be fatal.

Wide-eyed yet strangely calm, the deputy spoke, "I must revenge my death, Sheriff Hurst. Forgive me."

With ghostly pallor, the deputy lifted his sword and rushed to where Maddock lay.

"Maddock!" Edlyn shouted. "Maddock, look out!"

Just before the deputy reached his intended victim, Maddock opened his eyes and rolled out of the way. The deputy's sword came down on the stone floor with a violent clang. Maddock sprang to his feet, holding his dagger ready, but the deputy did not move to strike again. The deputy dropped his weapon, which fell to his feet with a clatter, and as blood continued to trickle from the wound in his heart, he collapsed.

"Ah," Sheriff Hurst's unaffected voice cut through the morbid silence. "Another deputy gone. This one was so devoted, too." He shook his head and sighed. "I shall have to get another one as soon as we get back to the castle."

"You are a monster," Edlyn spat, swinging one arm to try and strike her captor.

The sheriff only chuckled and put his arm more firmly around Edlyn's neck. He then glared vengefully at Maddock. "As for you, young man, you have created far too much disruption for my liking. I would enjoy killing you now. However, the king and queen are quite interested in meeting you, and I would be rewarded for bringing you to them. So you may choose: surrender, allowing me to take you back to the castle to be tortured and killed, or resist, forcing me to kill her and slaughter you immediately."

The sheriff emphasized his remarks by pressing his sword into Edlyn's side. Maddock flinched and lowered his dagger.

"Valiant choice," Sheriff Hurst told Maddock. "Now, let us—"

The sheriff broke off with a howl when Edlyn suddenly kicked him in the leg. She kicked again, and there was an audible, sickening crack as her boot struck his knee. Sheriff Hurst made another cry of pain, and his grip on Edlyn loosened.

"Get out of here, Maddock! Go now!" Edlyn yelled, twisting herself away from the sheriff and motioning to the door.

But instead, Maddock sprinted toward her, grabbed Edlyn by the wrist, and threw her aside. Edlyn landed on the ground, looking up just in time to see

Sheriff Hurst make an angry swipe with his sword where she had stood a moment before.

Maddock rammed himself into the sheriff's gut. Grunting from the impact, Sheriff Hurst dropped his weapon. Maddock made a lunge for the loose sword. The sheriff dove to stop him. There was a fierce struggle before Sheriff Hurst managed to grab the sword by the hilt and beat its pommel into Maddock's back. Thrown forward, Maddock lost hold of his dagger. Sheriff Hurst cackled victoriously and approached the unarmed Maddock to strike a final blow.

"Maddock, here!" Edlyn shouted, sliding Lord Faddin's sword across the floor.

The sword came within Maddock's reach as Sheriff Hurst pounced on him. Lifting the sword, Maddock repelled the sheriff's strike and pushed him backward.

"So you choose to fight and die," the sheriff hissed, regaining his balance.

Maddock got to his feet. "I do not want to fight, but I will if I must."

Sheriff Hurst smiled maliciously. "I cannot say that I am disappointed. I have wanted to kill you myself, and so I shall, here and now."

Maddock adjusted his stance and raised his weapon. "Very well. Let us—"

"Sheriff Hurst, drop your sword," Edlyn commanded.

Sheriff Hurst stopped, glanced at Edlyn, and then became very still. Maddock followed the sheriff's surprised gaze and nearly grinned.

Edlyn was standing close to the men, holding Maddock's dagger in one hand and the dead deputy's sword in the other. Eyes flashing, Edlyn pointed the sword directly at the sheriff's chest.

"I may be nothing but a servant girl to you, Sheriff Hurst, but I have been taught how to defend myself and am not afraid to do so," Edlyn declared.

The sheriff stared at her.

"Sheriff Hurst, if I am not mistaken, *you* are now the one who is injured and outnumbered," Maddock remarked wryly.

Sheriff Hurst narrowed his eyes, dropped his weapon, and threw his head back. "Then kill me swiftly, you traitors."

Edlyn used her foot to push the sheriff's sword out of reach. Keeping her weapons aloft, she stepped between the two men and faced the sheriff squarely. "If you make an oath never to hunt us, I will let you depart with your life."

"An oath?" Sheriff Hurst repeated mockingly. "I would rather die. So kill me, Edlyn. Kill the man who has offered to provide for you. Murder me in the name of protecting this outlaw, even though you have no idea why he is wanted. Rest assured, however, that as soon as you have enabled him to escape, this young man will disappear from your life."

Edlyn blinked hard. The tip of her sword remained where it was, but she did not strike.

Sheriff Hurst's expression was satisfied. "This outlaw cares nothing for you, Edlyn."

Maddock suddenly made an aggressive step around Edlyn to get at the sheriff.

"Stop, Maddock!" Edlyn cut him off, pointing the dagger warningly.

Maddock halted, clearly stunned. "Edlyn, what are you—"

"It is true, Maddock. I do not know what you are wanted for," she reminded him, trembling. "Are you also a murderer, no better than the sheriff?"

Maddock studied Edlyn for a long moment, and then he put down his sword. She kept watching him, her breathing strained and her mind racing.

Wounded and unarmed, Sheriff Hurst took the chance to make his escape. At the sound of him hefting aside the beam that had locked the door, Edlyn whipped around and faced him again.

"I appreciate you being so very accommodating, Edlyn," Sheriff Hurst stated with feigned politeness. "As soon I reach the town, I will gather the local garrison. I will then return for you, and I will hunt down and kill this outlaw. You, boy, will be sorry that you ever saw my face, and you, Edlyn, will be mine."

Sheriff Hurst quickly limped into the passageway and disappeared from view.

4

Edlyn finally lowered the sword, staring numbly at the two motionless bodies on the cold floor. It took a while before she realized that Maddock was saying something:

"Edlyn, we have to hurry. We must get rations and depart before Sheriff Hurst returns."

Edlyn could only nod.

"Keep the deputy's sword...and my dagger, if you would prefer," Maddock added with a strained gesture to the weapons that Edlyn still gripped in her hands. After snatching up Lord Faddin's sword himself, Maddock peered again at Edlyn, who remained silent. Eyes clouding with concern, he came to her side. "Edlyn, I am sorry about all of this. Are you well enough?"

"Yes, Maddock, I am well enough," she told him. She held out his dagger. "Thank you for saving me."

He slowly took the dagger and then placed his other hand firmly on her shoulder. "Edlyn, I cannot tell you everything about my past, but I swear that you have nothing to fear from me. I also swear that I will do all in my power to make this right for you. I am going to take you somewhere safe—somewhere you can start a new life. A better life. I promise."

"Do not worry for me," Edlyn replied, her strength renewing under his gaze. "I have no possessions and no family. I am not sad to go with you."

Maddock opened his mouth as if to say something more, but he instead grabbed Edlyn by the hand and led her out of the dining hall. They rushed down the serfs' passageway and burst into the kitchen.

Lancy sprang up from the table with an exclamation of alarm. When she saw Edlyn, she blotted tears away with her apron. "Miss Edlyn! I was so worried! I did not know what they had done to you! I..." She broke off and pointed to Maddock, seeming confused but not afraid. "Who is this?"

Edlyn ran to the woman and gripped her by the arms. "Dear Lancy, there is not time to explain everything, but Lord Faddin is dead and—"

"Dead!" Lancy repeated. "Lord Faddin is—"

"Lancy, you must listen!" Edlyn shouted, shaking her. "The sheriff has fled, but he will soon return with soldiers who are ordered to capture this young man and me. I am certain that Sheriff Hurst will destroy this manor and anyone who is still here when he comes. You must warn the other serfs, Lancy. Tell them to gather their things, take all the animals, and flee. Quickly! You are free, but you must go now!"

Lancy searched Edlyn's face. "What about you, miss?"

Edlyn blinked hard. "I do not think that I shall ever see you again."

Lancy threw her arms around Edlyn. Edlyn embraced her friend for only a moment before stepping back.

"Go, Lancy," Edlyn insisted, fighting her own tears. "Hurry."

With a final affectionate glance, Lancy sped from the kitchen.

Maddock immediately grabbed an empty hessian sack from the corner and tossed it to Edlyn. "Fill this with any supplies that you can find and meet me at the stable."

Without another word, Maddock ran past Edlyn and out the back door. Through the window, Edlyn saw him sprinting for the stable. She turned and charged to the other side of the kitchen, yanked open a door, and crossed into the deserted room beyond.

A stream of light coming through the partially covered window revealed that the large room was still littered with remnants of its former use, having once been the living quarters of several serfs. After the serfs were sold, the room became the classroom where Edlyn's father had taught her to create potions, use weapons, and read and write. It was the place where he told her of the Colleland and the Man in White. It was the room where she had listened to stories about her mother.

Standing in the doorway, countless tender memories of better times drifted through Edlyn's mind, but she quickly made herself put childhood remembrances aside and stepped farther into the room. Scavenging through dusty cupboards and armoires, Edlyn stuffed her hessian sack with clothing, blankets, bandages and other supplies, until she could carry no more. Then she paused, knowing that there was one more thing she needed to do.

In a corner of the room stood a wooden cabinet, which Edlyn had not opened in a very long time. Shaking slightly, she knelt in front of the cabinet, wiped dust from its surface, and pressed a hidden latch that opened the top drawer. Inside the drawer sat a green velvet bag. Gently, Edlyn picked up the small bag, untied its drawstring, and removed a necklace from inside.

Edlyn held the necklace up, fingering the triangle-shaped medallion that hung from the silver chain, which seemed to shine brightly despite the dimness of the room. The sight of the necklace took

Edlyn back to the night when her father had first shown it to her. The necklace once belonged to her mother, he had explained, and he instructed Edlyn to always protect it.

Wiping new tears away, Edlyn put on the necklace, concealing it under the collar of her dress. She then stuffed the velvet bag into her sack, put on a long cloak, and left the room.

Frantic shouting and commotion filled the manor house. The serfs who remained under Lord Faddin's ownership were hurrying to depart, taking with them the animals, food, and all else that they were able to gather. Edlyn wove through the chaos without speaking to anyone, headed outside, and ran to the stable.

"Maddock?" she called as she entered, finding the stable eerily empty and quiet. "Maddock, are you in here?"

Maddock emerged from a stall, leading a tall chestnut horse named Zanavian with one hand and Cynric with the other.

"The serfs gathered the other horses," he told Edlyn, holding out Cynric's reins for her to take. "But I kept these two for our use."

Edlyn hugged Cynric, who whinnied and nudged her in return. "Maddock," she asked, "how did you know to keep this one for me?"

"It was in the horse's eyes."

Edlyn peered at Maddock curiously, but he seemed not to notice and only motioned toward the stable door.

"We are in for a long and difficult journey, Edlyn."

She tightened her hold on Cynric's reins. "I am not afraid."

Maddock seemed to linger for a long moment before leading Zanavian from the stable. Edlyn followed, guiding Cynric into the late-morning sunlight. She easily swung herself up on the horse's back and cast a final look at the emptied manor house. Gazing for the last time upon the only home she had ever known, Edlyn's throat caught unexpectedly. Yet although a myriad of emotions coursed through her heart, neither sadness nor regret was among them. As a breeze began to stir, Edlyn's thoughts shifted from her past to her unknown future. She turned to the young man on the horse beside her.

"Where will we go, Maddock? The mountains?"

The wind tousled his hair. "No. That is exactly what Sheriff Hurst will expect, and he will send soldiers first into the mountains to track us down. On that terrain, with so many after us, we would not be able to outrun them all."

"Then what are we going to do?"

"Today, we are going to travel in the only direction Sheriff Hurst will not think to look for us. We will go toward the castle."

"*Toward* the castle?" Edlyn repeated, her stomach lurching.

"Yes. We will use Ravenshire Forest for cover and keep close to the river. Tomorrow, with the sheriff off our trail, I will be able to get you to a place that is safe."

Edlyn instinctively fingered the sword at her side. "They say that Ravenshire Forest is enchanted."

"Or haunted, depending upon what you..." Maddock broke off and looked past her. "Sheriff Hurst and the soldiers from town are coming."

Edlyn checked over her shoulder. She saw nothing. Confused, she continued scanning the distant fields until she finally noticed what Maddock's keen eye had already spotted. Far off, on the long road that led up to the manor, a small cloud of dust was barely visible. Edlyn knew that such a cloud could only be caused by a group of horsemen.

"Edlyn, we must ride," she heard Maddock say.

Pulse quickening, Edlyn looked at Maddock again. He pointed Zanavian in the direction of Ravenshire Forest. Edlyn made Cynric do the same. As the horses whinnied excitedly, Edlyn gave Maddock a nod. He nodded back. Then they began riding at full gallop from the manor, side by side.

Over the ground they flew, headed directly into the wind with the steady sound of their horses' hooves accompanying their flight. The horses seemed to sense the urgency of the journey; keeping their heads down, the animals did not falter as they pounded the dirt to carry their riders away from the manor.

On and on they went, the scenery becoming a blur as they continued racing through the uninhabited countryside for Ravenshire Forest. Edlyn's eyes stung, and her cloak whipped in the crisp breeze. But although she and Maddock kept their eyes forward, their ears remained focused behind them. They both knew that they vulnerable while crossing the open fields. At any moment, a soldier might spot them. They were in a life-or-death race for cover.

More agonizing time passed. Edlyn did not know how far they had traveled when the trees of Ravenshire Forest finally appeared on the horizon. At the sight, Maddock made another sharp call to his steed. Zanavian, the strongest of Lord Faddin's horses, easily increased her pace at Maddock's command. Edlyn crouched low, making a clicking sound in Cynric's ear, and her faithful animal responded by also picking up his speed.

Overhead, clouds rolled in front of the sun, dimming the sky from blue to gray. As the riders drew closer to the forest, the land over which they traveled became rocky, causing the horses to slow down.

"When we are within the cover of the forest, we will stop to let the horses rest!" Maddock called out.

Edlyn did not respond to him. Watching the forest, something powerful—something that she could not explain—had begun stirring within her. She became more aware of her mother's necklace, which swayed against her body as she rode, and she had the strange sense that the ancient, towering trees were awaiting their arrival.

An instant later, Edlyn was jarred from her thoughts when she and Maddock crossed from the open field into the cover of Ravenshire Forest. Everything became dark and quiet. Slowing their pace, they rode deeper into the thick trees, the sound of the horses' steps muted by the lush ground underfoot. They continued eastward, dodging the branches, moss-covered stumps, and hidden roots in their path. When they entered a small clearing, Maddock signaled to bring the horses to a stop.

"Stay on your horse, Edlyn," he said, dismounting Zanavian.

Maddock began searching their surroundings, his movements silent and deliberate. Remaining atop her horse, Edlyn peered about while keeping one hand on the hilt of her sword. She saw that the gigantic, knotted trees completely encircled the clearing, their massive branches stretching up to the sky and creating a thick ceiling overhead. Edlyn squinted into the dimness beyond the trees with both curiosity and trepidation. She had never ventured into Ravenshire Forest, but she had often heard tales of the mystical creatures that dwelt within.

"There is fire in the air," Maddock announced. "The manor house is burning. Sheriff Hurst has begun his destruction."

Edlyn breathed in deeply but only detected scents of the forest. She put her eyes on Maddock, studying him with admiration. "The manor house is very far away, yet you can detect new flames already. Your senses are sharp, Maddock."

He did not reply as he mounted his horse. Gathering the reins in one hand, he motioned to his left. "The river is this way. We must water the horses now so we can be back within the cover of the forest by nightfall."

Edlyn did not argue, letting Maddock lead the way—a way he seemed instinctively to know. Several minutes passed before Edlyn began hearing the sound of moving water, which was followed by growing glimpses of daylight between the trees. Before long, they emerged from the forest and approached the edge of the river.

"What about Sheriff Hurst?" Edlyn questioned uneasily as she looked around the exposed riverbank. "Rather than set up camp, should we not continue riding to outrun him?"

Maddock shook his head. "Sheriff Hurst is only one of our concerns. There are many dangers lurking in this part of the land. We would be unwise to travel after dusk."

Edlyn shivered. "You do not think that Sheriff Hurst will find us here?"

"Not tonight." Maddock got down from his horse. "We are lucky that he was foolish enough to use fire as his weapon. It will make it impossible for his hunting dogs to track our scent. Once the soldiers destroyed the manor and found we were not there, Sheriff Hurst undoubtedly led them to the Fierlen

Mountains to search for us. It will be nightfall before they realize that their quest is futile. They will go to the castle by the regular roads to rest and regroup. So tonight, we will be safe from them here."

While Maddock spoke, he had walked over to Cynric's side. Before Edlyn realized what he was doing, Maddock reached up, put his hands on Edlyn's waist, and lifted her down to the ground. Stunned, Edlyn raised her eyes to his. Maddock let go of her and stepped back.

"Your horse is thirsty," he stated.

Edlyn blinked. "What?"

Maddock took Zanavian by the reins and led the animal to the water. "You should let your horse drink now."

"Yes...yes, of course," Edlyn stammered.

Hands trembling, Edlyn guided Cynric to the deep river. Sunlight began poking through the clouds, causing the water to sparkle a deep, vibrant green as it coursed lazily past. While Cynric drank, Edlyn hid herself behind the horse so that she was out of Maddock's view. Taking a slow breath, she stared restlessly at the steep bank on the opposite side of the river.

Never would Edlyn have predicted that she was capable of feeling the way she did at that moment. Yet, try as she might, she could not deny that the enigmatic young man from the Colleland was stirring something within her heart that she had never felt before—something both wonderful and frightening.

However, Edlyn knew that she could not dwell on such sentiments. A man from the Colleland had murdered her father, and on that terrible night, Edlyn had vowed to dedicate her life to hunting down the killer and revenging her father's death. Edlyn would not betray her father's memory by giving in to fleeting, fanciful emotion.

Cynric snorted contentedly, bringing Edlyn to herself once again. To her relief, the spell that had seemed to be upon her was broken—her disconcerting feelings for Maddock were suppressed and her resolution restored. Reaching out, Edlyn began stroking Cynric's mane.

Her hands, she realized, were filthy.

"Maddock?" She poked her head under Cynric's neck so that she could see him. "How much time do we have before nightfall?"

Maddock checked the sky. "Two hours."

"Then I need you to step away and turn around."

"What?"

"I need you to step away and turn around," Edlyn repeated. "I am going to take a bath."

"A bath?" he echoed as if not certain he was hearing her correctly.

"Yes. Since this may be the last chance we have to easily access clean water for a while, I want to take advantage of it. We will still have plenty of time to set up camp for the night."

His mouth dropped open slightly.

"Go on," Edlyn said, waving dismissively at him. "The longer you delay, the less time we will have."

Maddock kept a bewildered eye on her for a few seconds more and then tied Zanavian to a tree. He walked to a large boulder and sat down, facing away from her.

"Alright, Edlyn. I am...situated."

"Good. Although when I am done, you should consider taking a bath yourself, Maddock. I can only imagine how long it has been since you properly cleaned up."

He sat up straight. "What?"

Edlyn giggled and lifted off the heavy sword that hung at her side, setting it on the ground. A soft wind swayed the trees on the riverbank as she removed her long cloak and draped it over Cynric. She next stepped out of her worn dress, the sting of the fabric against the whip marks on her back a vivid reminder of the world she had so recently left behind. Once the discomfort subsided, Edlyn waded into the river, immersing her body in its refreshing current. She swam underwater from the shore and floated again to the surface.

"Maddock, the water is very pleasant. You should take a swim when I am done," she called to him.

"I would rather not," he replied, still facing the other way.

"But the water is—"

"I do not know how to swim."

Edlyn paused, treading water. "Surely you are not serious."

"I surely am."

"Then I shall have to teach you to swim one day," Edlyn concluded. "But I must admit that I am shocked, Maddock. I thought there was nothing you did not know."

"Then you have been drastically mistaken."

From the tone in his voice, Edlyn surmised that he was smiling—and, Edlyn realized, she was smiling, too. Quickly, she tipped her head back and closed her eyes, trying to distract herself. With the sunshine warming her face, she made a few more lazy strokes, and then she raised her head and reopened her eyes.

"Alright, Maddock. I am going to come out now."

He cleared his throat. "Yes. Very...very well."

As Edlyn turned to the shore, she saw a movement within the trees. A moment later, she saw another flash of motion.

Someone—or something—was watching them.

5

"Maddock, there is something in the trees!"

Maddock sprang up and spun toward the forest, his dagger raised. "Edlyn, stay where you are!" he shouted over his shoulder.

But Edlyn ignored Maddock's command and began paddling for land. When she neared the shore, she whistled for Cynric, who came charging into the water. As the horse reached her, Edlyn felt the riverbed beneath her feet. She stood, yanked her long cloak down from the horse's back, and tied the garment around her body. Breathing hard, she scrambled for her sword, which sat on the riverbank, and then raced to Maddock's side.

"Edlyn," Maddock sharply said in a low voice, "Take Cynric and hide. Quickly. If anything happens to me, you ride north as fast as you can. Do you understand?"

She looked up at him, the water from her wet hair rolling down her face. "What I do is my choice, Maddock, not yours. I will not leave you here alone. "

"Edlyn, there are things in the forest that—"

A twig snapped. Maddock and Edlyn both turned anxiously toward the noise, weapons ready. All was still except for the rustling leaves. Seconds passed. Zanavian stomped her hooves. Cynric snorted.

After another glance at Edlyn, Maddock slid forward until he was up to the edge of the forest. He paused, and Edlyn knew that he was searching with eyes that saw what others could not and listening for things no one else discerned. Adjusting his grip on his dagger, Maddock then stepped into the shadows.

Unexpectedly, a piercing musical noise rang through the air. Edlyn shouted in surprise and instinctively ducked, covering her head with her arms. She heard the sound of Maddock grunting in pain followed by something landing hard on the ground nearby. Edlyn dropped her arms. To her alarm, it was Maddock who was sprawled on the dirt beside her.

"Maddock!" Edlyn shrieked.

He held up an arm, signaling that he was alright. "I thought as much," he grumbled, getting to his feet. He spoke loudly toward the trees, "I am not frightened. I know that your powers are strong only when you are in the forest. You cannot harm me if I am on the riverbank."

"Yes, but you cannot be safe unless you are in the forest. So it appears that we are at a draw, does it not, Fugitive?" came a voice from the forest in reply.

Edlyn faced the trees, astonished. "Who is there?"

"I was going to ask you the same question," answered the voice.

"Do not bother trying to carry on a rational conversation," Maddock told Edlyn with annoyance. "It is a Langerlan. He will enjoy trying to frustrate you."

Edlyn's mouth fell open. "A Langerlan? They exist?"

"Of course we exist," the voice replied, indignant.

"Elusive creatures," Maddock added, repositioning the dagger in his hand.

"Elusive? You are the one who tried sneaking into the forest, Fugitive," the Langerlan pointed out.

Maddock stopped, a perturbed expression appearing on his face.

"The Langerlan *is* right, Maddock," Edlyn commented with a laugh. "They are supposed to guard Ravenshire Forest, are they not? We are the ones who came unannounced."

"A young woman of reason," the Langerlan declared.

"Thank you," Edlyn told the thing that remained hidden. After giving Maddock another look, she concealed her smile and stepped nearer to the forest. "My name is Edlyn. This is Maddock. We are seeking refuge for the night. We hope that you will allow us this."

"You have weapons," observed the voice.

"Yes." Edlyn nodded. "Those on our trail seek to do us harm."

"Hmm. I am curious to learn who is after you." The Langerlan seemed to think. "Ah-ha! I know! You two are in love and eloping, and now your family is after you. They intend to kill this fugitive and make you wed someone else. Is that right?"

Edlyn blushed. "No, we are not in love. We are being hunted by Sheriff Hurst."

"Sheriff Hurst?" The Langerlan sounded intrigued. "What have done to gain his attention?"

Edlyn gestured to Maddock, letting her smile show. "I am not sure, for Maddock will not tell me. But I can attest to the fact that Sheriff Hurst most certainly wants to take his life."

"I should have known," the Langerlan remarked. "He is stubborn, hard to reason with, and angry."

"You sound as though you know the sheriff well," Edlyn stated, surprised.

"I was referring to the fugitive with whom you travel," the Langerlan responded bluntly.

Maddock grumbled something under his breath. Edlyn dropped her head, stifling another laugh.

"So, Fugitive, Sheriff Hurst is after you, is he?" the Langerlan resumed, addressing Maddock. "Why does—"

"Look, Langerlan, we do not have much time," Maddock cut in. "Banter with me all you want, but let Edlyn have shelter for the night. She has done nothing wrong."

There was a pause.

"I believe that is a reasonable request," the Langerlan decided. "Very well. Come forward, young lady. You are allowed entrance."

"Thank you, but I cannot accept your offer," she replied politely. "I will not go unless Maddock is able to receive shelter, too."

Maddock stepped close to her. "Edlyn, it is growing late. Take the horses and set up camp. I can manage by myself."

She crossed her arms. "As I said before, I will not leave you."

"And I will not let you put yourself in more danger," Maddock replied firmly.

"Interesting, indeed," the Langerlan remarked while Maddock and Edlyn eyed each other. "Perhaps there is something redeeming in you yet, Fugitive. Very well, you both may enter and find the shelter you seek."

Giving Maddock a satisfied look, Edlyn turned and went to Cynric's side. She put her sword away, collected her things, and began leading the horse toward the forest. Maddock still had his weapon drawn as he brought Zanavian up beside her.

"Keep a wary eye out," he advised. "Do not trust the inhabitants of this forest."

"I understand," Edlyn assured him, though she did fear the unseen creature.

When they reached the trees, Edlyn and Maddock exchanged a glance before reentering the darkness. Maddock's eyes immediately began scanning the shadows around them. Edlyn, too, gazed about and listened hard, and she was almost disappointed to note nothing peculiar.

"Come," Maddock soon said, motioning for Edlyn to follow.

The sound of the river faded as they moved farther into the forest. Daylight disappeared, the sky again becoming hidden by trees overhead. After a short journey, Maddock brought them to a stop.

"We should set up camp here."

Still barefoot, Edlyn examined the choice of refuge for the night. They were in a level clearing that was enclosed by dense foliage. Satisfied, Edlyn tied Cynric to a tree and began searching the satchels that hung over the horse's back.

"I have the supplies for our shelters," she reported, turning to Maddock. "We can..."

Edlyn trailed off. Standing right behind Maddock was a man—or, rather, a creature.

Before Edlyn could say anything, Maddock was already in motion. As if he had sensed the thing's presence, Maddock whipped around and threw himself into it, knocking it flat on its back.

"I knew you were tracking us." Maddock pointed his dagger at the creature's neck. "Who are you?"

"Maddock, do not hurt it!" Edlyn yelled, running to his side.

"Yes, the young woman is indeed proving to be the more reasonable one of the pair," the creature stated.

Edlyn halted upon hearing the familiar voice. It was the Langerlan.

Maddock sat back and released his hold upon the creature, but he did not lower his dagger.

As the thing got to his feet, Edlyn observed him incredulously. In some ways, he looked like a human, yet he was most certainly a creature of another kind. He was extremely short, and his eyes glowed vibrant green. His nose was long and straight, his skin pale, and his hair and beard were bright blue. The hat and robe that the Langerlan wore were made of intricately woven leaves and branches.

"Hello, Langerlan," Edlyn greeted him, fascinated. "What is your name?"

"I am Kegan," he replied importantly. "I will attend to you tonight."

Maddock put his weapon away. "We do not need you here."

"It does not matter what you think you need, Fugitive," Kegan replied. "I am ordered to attend you, and so I shall."

Maddock stopped. "Ordered? By whom?"

"You keep secrets, and I will, too," Kegan retorted matter-of-factly.

With a roll of his eyes, Maddock moved past the Langerlan and began taking his things down from Zanavian's back. "As I said, we do not need your help."

Kegan scurried after him. "Only a fool would think that. You will not be safe without help. There are traitors within this forest who would readily disclose your location to those who are hunting you."

"I know of the dangers here, Langerlan."

Kegan sighed. "Very stubborn. Now I see why I was told to keep such a close watch on you."

Maddock only shook his head.

"Maddock, surely there are things about this forest that we do not know. No doubt Kegan can be of great service to us," Edlyn suggested, and she gave the Langerlan an apologetic smile. "We thank you for your help."

Kegan bowed to her. "You are most welcome. It is a pleasure to assist *you*, at least."

"I have long heard stories about the Langerlen," Edlyn went on excitedly. "I am greatly interested in learning more about you."

Kegan proudly puffed out his chest. "And I would be greatly pleased to tell you. Please, sit down."

Edlyn gladly obeyed, situating herself on a large tree stump. Standing up as tall as he could, Kegan began his tale:

"The Langerlen are some of the most ancient inhabitants of this land. We were here long before those such as you traveled the earth. While we now hide within this forest, we once roamed freely. But when King Whittemoor died, we, like all others loyal to Tiernan, had no choice but to flee or go into hiding. So we gathered here in Ravenshire Forest, our original home, where our powers are the strongest."

Edlyn wrapped her cloak tightly around her as she listened. She noticed that Maddock had slowed what he was doing, but if he was paying attention to the Langerlan's tale, Edlyn could not tell.

Kegan continued, "The curse of King Whittemoor's daughter, Raelin, fell over the land. No one in Nereth could escape, and no one who had fled to the Colleland with Tiernan could return. Guthrie soon waged war upon all in Nereth who did not swear allegiance to the king and queen. We Langerlen had no choice but to remain hidden here. Since that time, we have guarded the forest, aided those who sought to fight evil, and awaited the day when Tiernan's descendent will claim the throne."

"Forgive me for interrupting," Maddock called out with a hint of impatience. "It is growing late, and we must finish setting up camp."

Kegan strolled to Maddock's side. "You do not believe the ancient stories, do you, Fugitive? You consider the story of Tiernan and his descendents to be nothing but folk tales?"

Maddock was about to reply when he reached for his dagger and started sprinting for Edlyn. "Run!" he shouted to her.

Edlyn had no chance to react before something heavy pounced on her from behind. She was hurled to the ground, face-first, and pinned down. Edlyn heard a terrible growling noise, and sharp claws began scratching her neck. She struggled to get away, but the thing that was upon her had immense strength. Dirt soon filled her nose and mouth. She could not breathe.

The sound of Maddock's racing footsteps got close, and then the thing that was attacking Edlyn let out a horrible shriek. Its grip released. Edlyn crawled out from underneath it and staggered to her feet. To her shock, she saw Maddock crouching over a large animal that had yellow eyes and thick black fur. Salivating and growling, the monster snapped its massive jaws at Maddock, revealing jagged teeth.

Maddock raised his weapon to deal the beast a fatal blow when another yellow-eyed animal emerged from the trees and leapt into the fray. Edlyn screamed a warning as the second beast came down on Maddock. She heard the sounds of ripping clothes and flesh, and then Maddock let out a yell of pain. Desperate, Edlyn picked up a large stone and hurled it at one of the monsters, striking it hard in the head. The wounded animal fell backward, allowing Maddock to break free. Edlyn immediately turned and dashed for her sword, which was still hanging over Cynric's back. As she grabbed her weapon, the horse unexpectedly reared up with fright. Then Edlyn heard something behind her let out an awful growl. Throat tight, she turned around.

Edlyn found herself staring directly into the yellow eyes of yet another of the terrifying beasts. Pupils dilated and mouth salivating, it began steadily approaching. Edlyn gripped her sword and readied herself, her ears still ringing with the agonizing sounds of Maddock fighting the other animals alone. Edlyn made one anxious scan of the clearing. Kegan was gone.

There was another low growl from the monster that was stalking Edlyn. She stared back at it, her heart pounding, as the beast's hungry, yellow eyes focused on her neck. Slowly, Edlyn reached out her free arm and untied Cynric from the tree. She then gathered her footing, timing her strike. When the beast took another step closer, Edlyn thrust her sword forward. She struck the thing in its chest, causing it to let out a howl. As Edlyn raised her sword to swing again, the beast lunged for her.

Suddenly, the air resonated again with a strange melodic sound. The animal was hurled away from Edlyn, as if struck by an unseen force. Astounded, Edlyn turned her head in the direction from which the unworldly noise had come. Kegan was there, holding a glass sphere in his hand.

"Strike now," the Langerlan commanded her.

Edlyn obeyed, rushing the stunned beast and driving her sword skillfully into its chest. "Kegan, we must help Maddock!" Edlyn yelled, pulling her sword from the corpse.

Without waiting for the Langerlan, Edlyn bolted across the clearing to where Maddock continued his battle. Maddock's movements were barely visible underneath the two massive animals that attacked him. Edlyn lifted her sword, about to charge, when the unusual sound rang out again—but this time from somewhere deep within the trees. Immediately, one of the beasts let out a wail, flung to the dirt by an invisible impact. With her sword still aloft, Edlyn took the chance to kill the monster before it could recover. Yanking her weapon free, Edlyn looked back and let out a shout of relief.

Maddock had escaped from the last animal's hold. Shirt torn and blood streaming down his left arm, Maddock was circling the beast, which snarled and paced as it watched him. Edlyn sprinted upon it from behind, slashing the monster in its side. Maddock then drove his dagger into its chest. The animal's breathing stopped, and its yellow eyes closed.

A shocked quiet followed.

Letting his dagger fall from his grip, Maddock dropped to his knees. He leaned forward, resting with his hands on the ground. "Are you alright?" he asked Edlyn, wearily raising his head.

Stunned and shaking, Edlyn approached him. "Yes, Maddock, I am alright."

Maddock turned to Kegan, who was coming toward them. "Thank you, Langerlan. It appears that we greatly needed your help, after all."

Kegan gave Maddock a bow. "You are most welcome, Fugitive."

Maddock refocused on Edlyn. "And it seems that, once again, I needed your help, too. Thank you, Edlyn."

Edlyn watched Maddock, her heart so full of emotion that she wondered if it might burst. But she kept her feelings to herself, responding to him only with:

"We should go back to camp, Maddock. I must tend to your injury."

Maddock lifted his bloodied left arm. "It is not serious."

"I certainly hope that is the case," Edlyn replied, her voice still not quite even, "but I need to check, nonetheless. We must hurry. The sun is going down."

Maddock observed her for a second or two, and then he stood and walked off toward their camp. Edlyn remained behind, watching him go.

"You told me before that you were not in love," Kegan remarked to her.

Edlyn quickly faced him. "That is the truth. I am not in love. I will never be in love."

She did not allow the Langerlan to reply, turning abruptly and heading after Maddock. Upon reaching the clearing, Edlyn was met by a dismal sight: their supplies had been scattered and badly trampled during the fight. With a cry of dismay, Edlyn crouched down and began sorting through dirtied blankets, bent tools, and spilled water flasks to assess the damage.

"I found some of our clothing over here," Maddock shouted.

Edlyn spotted Maddock on the other side of the clearing, retrieving what he could with his good arm.

"Maddock, you should rest," Edlyn called out, placing food back into a satchel. "I can finish this."

He came toward her, using one arm to carry what he had gathered, and grinned slightly. "While the clothing is surely too dirty for your liking, Edlyn, I am glad to report that our supplies have not been destroyed completely."

Try as she might, Edlyn could not prevent a smile from appearing on her own face. "We are lucky, indeed. Now sit down and let me care for your arm."

Maddock opened his mouth as if to protest but then seemed to think better of it. He sat down and leaned against a tree. A moment later, though, he lifted his head once again. "Where are the horses?"

As if in response, there came a familiar whinny from near the clearing. Edlyn and Maddock looked toward the sound and saw Cynric, his reins hanging freely, standing protectively beside Zanavian.

"They are alright!" Edlyn exclaimed joyfully.

"Of course they are alright," Kegan remarked, walking over with a pile of their blankets in his arms. "The horses were not what those monsters were after." He looked squarely at Maddock. "That was no ordinary attack, Fugitive. Evil forces were at work here. Those beasts wanted you dead."

"I seem to have a habit of making people and things want to kill me," Maddock quipped.

Edlyn did not laugh. She drenched a cloth in water, crouched beside Maddock, and began blotting away the blood on his left arm. "Kegan, do you mean that those horrible monsters worked for the sheriff?"

Kegan shook his head. "No, Sheriff Hurst does not have such powers. Those were Berax—animals whose loyalty is to the king and queen alone. They are spies that roam the forest. It is good they are dead, otherwise your whereabouts would have been reported and your journey short, indeed."

Edlyn shuddered and kept cleaning the claw marks on Maddock's arm.

Maddock leaned his head in close, trying to see what she was doing. "Edlyn, what do you make of the wound?"

"Thankfully, you were right," she told him, very aware of how near his face was to hers. "The injury is not as bad as I feared."

Maddock nodded and sat back again. Edlyn steadied her breathing and continued her work. A soothing breeze stirred the trees, and a calmness settled over the group. After a while, Edlyn addressed the Langerlan:

"Kegan, you were not the only one who helped us fight the Berax, were you? I heard another sound from the woods while Maddock was fighting."

When Kegan did not answer, Edlyn glanced over at him. She realized that the Langerlan's green eyes were fixed upon the symbol that was exposed on Maddock's left shoulder.

"Fugitive," Kegan uttered, "you are from the Colleland."

Maddock dropped his head resignedly. "Yes. So if you intend to kick me out of the forest, please tell me now. I would appreciate having time to make shelter before nightfall."

"Fugitive, you are from the Colleland," Kegan repeated in nearly a whisper.

Maddock slowly raised his head. Kegan knelt down and peered at him.

"Fugitive, are you The One?"

Edlyn glanced confusedly between them, but as understanding struck her, she gasped softly and studied Maddock anew. Maddock was from the Colleland, and he was in Nereth despite Raelin's ancient curse. Was it possible that the young man beside her was the one spoken of in ancient legend? Was Maddock the descendent of Tiernan and rightful heir to the throne, as described to her father by the Man in White? Was Maddock destined to unite the Kingdom of Nereth?

Maddock was still watching Kegan, his expression unchanged. "No, Langerlan, I am not the one you await."

"But you are in Nereth," Kegan went on in a tone of awe. "You were able to enter the kingdom. You somehow—"

"Raelin's curse has a weakness," Maddock interrupted. "I am not the only one who has discovered this. Others from the Colleland have entered Nereth before me, and surely more will do so." He looked quickly at Edlyn. "Believe me, I am no hero of prophecy."

Kegan went on, "But, Maddock, whatever brings you here is enough for the king and queen to want you dead. Your quest must be—"

"Your quest, Maddock, is more burden than one young man should bear by himself," a different voice remarked.

Edlyn cried out with surprise, and Maddock jumped to his feet. Calmly, Kegan faced the trees and bowed. From the woods, a new figure emerged. Edlyn found herself staring in amazement at another Langerlan—a female who, like Kegan, had glowing green eyes. Her shimmering blue hair flowed freely down her back, and she, too, was dressed in an earthen robe.

Maddock put down his weapon.

The Langerlan woman surveyed the group and then addressed Kegan, "You were wise to bring me here when they were attacked. These two are hunted even more fiercely than we anticipated."

"I am glad we returned in time," Kegan replied somberly.

The Langerlan woman next spoke to Maddock, "I am Ailith, the ruler of the Langerlen. You are Maddock from the Colleland."

Maddock raised his eyebrows in surprise.

Ailith shifted her green eyes to Edlyn. "You have traveled far from home, Edlyn."

"You know my name," Edlyn uttered in wonderment.

"The forest speaks," Ailith replied, gesturing to the trees, "and the forest has been watching you."

Edlyn slowly looked around at the darkened wood, something stirring again within her heart.

Ailith smiled serenely. "Let us get you two situated for the night. We have much to talk about."

6

"Take this. The drink will do you good."

Edlyn gratefully accepted the wooden cup that Ailith held out to her, and she took a sip of the hot, violet-colored liquid it contained. As delicious warmth began filling her body, Edlyn reached for the blanket that hung over her shoulders and drew it close. For the first time in a very long while, Edlyn sensed herself truly relax.

Around her, the mysterious nighttime sounds of the forest floated in the air. The sky had grown dark, and the only remaining light came from the smokeless fire of blue flames that burned at the center of their camp.

"This fire cannot be seen by those outside the forest," Kegan had told Edlyn when he created the flames by brushing his hand against nothing but a cold stone. "It will keep you protected and warm tonight."

As promised, the fire had continued burning brightly, enveloping the camp with a comfortable, reassuring heat. Edlyn gazed upon the flames, sensing herself growing pleasantly sleepy. Taking another sip of her drink, she began watching the shadows of the fire dance upon the tents nearby.

Ailith placed unfamiliar food at Edlyn's side. "Eat this as well. I do not think you have had enough nutrition in recent days."

Edlyn sat up. "I admit that I am hungry."

"It was one of many noble sacrifices you made, going without your meals," Ailith remarked. She motioned to Maddock's tent. "I believe he understands what you did for him, and I think your actions have impacted him deeply."

"It proved to be the least that I could do," she explained to the Langerlan woman. "Maddock saved me from a fate worse than death. I am obviously happy to have helped him."

Ailith only smiled in response, and Edlyn had the disconcerting feeling that the Langerlan woman could read her deepest thoughts. After a time, Ailith went on:

"I see you wear a necklace, Edlyn. It is important to you, is it not?"

"It was my mother's." Edlyn tucked the exposed chain back under her collar. "I promised my father that I would always keep it safe."

"That is wise," Ailith said, returning to her place on the other side of the fire. "Now I shall cease with questions and let you eat."

Edlyn carefully lifted some food and took a small bite. She chewed slowly, savoring the rich flavors that were unlike anything she had ever tasted. Then, with a delighted sigh, Edlyn dove fully into her meal. Only once her hungry stomach had been satisfied did she look again at the Langerlen.

"I have wanted to ask something," Edlyn told them. "We talk much about the fate of King Whittemoor's banished son, Tiernan. But what happened to the king's daughter, Raelin, and younger son, Guthrie? After they ruled over the kingdom, how did their stories end?"

Kegan promptly stood up. "I shall be most pleased to answer. You see, after Tiernan and his followers fled from Nereth, Raelin put a curse upon this kingdom. The curse kept all in Nereth trapped within its boundaries, and it was also intended to prevent

Tiernan, his followers, and their descendents from ever returning to this land. It was said that the curse made the borders of Nereth impossible to find. There are even stories of some from the Colleland who tried to find Nereth but wandered until they died."

Edlyn nodded. "I have heard those tales. But what about Raelin and Guthrie? What happened to them?"

Kegan's eyes brightened. "Not many years after the curse was put upon this land, rumors began to be spoken. Quiet rumors. Rumors hinting that Raelin's curse had a weakness. You see, some in Nereth claimed to have seen one from the Colleland—a person they simply called the Man in White. Of course, speculation abounded as to why this man had been able to return despite the curse, but no one knew for certain."

Edlyn leaned forward, new questions filling her mind. "So what about others?"

"Others?" Kegan repeated, confused.

"Yes," Edlyn tried not to sound impatient. "Others from the Colleland who, over the centuries, also broke through Raelin's curse and returned to Nereth. Please tell me what you know about them."

"Edlyn, the curse of Raelin remains strong. Besides the Man in White, no others have been able to return from the Colleland." Kegan gestured toward Maddock's tent. "At least, not until the fugitive came across the border."

"No, Maddock is not the only other one," Edlyn insisted. "There was at least one more from the Colleland who came to Nereth. I saw him myself. He was here six years ago, and I must find him."

Kegan shot Ailith a quick look before smiling sympathetically at Edlyn. "You are worn out. We can talk about this another time."

Edlyn did not respond and hastily blinked away frustrated tears. No matter what others said, Edlyn was certain that her father's murderer had been from the Colleland. Though it had been too dark for her to see the killer's face on that horrid night, by the candlelight she had identified the unmistakable symbol of the Colleland on the man's shoulder.

Edlyn broke from her thoughts when she realized that Ailith was still observing her.

"Edlyn, what is the reason that you so keenly seek another from the Colleland?" the Langerlan woman inquired.

"There is no reason," Edlyn lied. "I am sure Kegan is right. I am just very tired."

Edlyn faked a smile and looked away, telling herself to be patient. One day, she would track down her father's killer. One day, she would revenge his death.

Lost in her thoughts, Edlyn did not notice that Maddock had stepped out from his tent until he was standing beside her. She glanced up at him, did a double take, and stared.

Maddock's thick hair had been washed, causing it to shine the firelight. His face was shaven, and the clean clothes he wore were well-fitted for his strong frame. Most notably, Maddock's dark eyes, which caught the reflection of the fire's blue flames, were peaceful.

"Is something the matter?" Maddock asked, nearly smiling.

Edlyn shook her head awkwardly. "No. You just look...different, that is all."

"Well, it is your doing," he replied, letting his grin show.

"*My* doing?"

"Yes. When we were at the river, you inferred that it had likely been some time since I properly cleaned up, did you not? So I took your remark as a challenge, and I cleaned up."

Edlyn laughed, grateful that it was dark so Maddock would not be able to see how she was blushing.

"Take this, Maddock," Ailith said, coming around the campfire and handing him food. "Eat well. From what you say, you have a long journey still."

Edlyn abruptly put her cup down. "Maddock, am I the only one here who does not know what mission brings you from the Colleland?"

Maddock glanced at Ailith, who returned his look but did not intercede. Maddock seemed to collect his thoughts before he faced Edlyn and answered her:

"As I said, Edlyn, I do not want to involve you in this more than necessary. What I am doing is not your concern, and I—"

"Not my concern?" Edlyn snapped. "You cannot be serious. Of course this is my concern. You may have started out on your journey alone, Maddock, but whether you like it or not, you are alone no longer. We have learned much of each other. I have saved your life, and you have saved mine. Sheriff Hurst is after us both. How can you say that this is not my concern?"

Letting her sharp words hang in the night air, Edlyn sat back and crossed her arms.

"Maddock, I cannot say what is best for you," Ailith remarked after a moment, "and your reason for maintaining secrecy is admirable, but perhaps Edlyn is right. Perhaps this journey is hers now, too. Perhaps, for reasons we may not fully understand, you should share your burden."

A thrill stirred within Edlyn's breast as she heard the Langerlan woman's words. Though she did not know why, Edlyn was certain that Ailith was right.

But Maddock's expression was set. "I cannot bring Edlyn into this. If I do, she will never have a normal life."

Edlyn put a hand on Maddock's arm. "I think it is already too late for me to have a normal life. After all, I am on the run from Sheriff Hurst, I have struck Berax down with a sword, and I now find myself in Ravenshire Forest eating with Langerlen. It is clear that my life is normal no longer."

Maddock only seemed more bothered by her words. "You deserve far better than this, Edlyn. I swear that I will free you from this and make things right."

"How? By abandoning me at the first village we come across?" Edlyn tossed her braid over her shoulder. "Maybe I do not want to be free from this, Maddock. Besides, no matter how much you insist otherwise, we both know that I never *will* be free from it."

Maddock said nothing.

Sensing she was getting through to him, Edlyn continued, "I want to know, Maddock, and I believe that I am supposed to know. Please."

It was a long time before Maddock looked at Edlyn again. There was a defeated—though calm—expression behind his eyes. With a slow breath, he began his tale:

"I was born in the Colleland. Like everyone else, I grew up hearing of Nereth, the land from where our people came. I was taught of noble King Whittemoor and the unrest among his children when he died. We learned that his son, Tiernan, had been forced to flee Nereth with his family and followers. I also learned of Raelin's curse, which prevented those in the Colleland from returning to Nereth. Many were the stories about those who sought to find Nereth but were never heard from again."

Maddock spoke steadily. Edlyn watched him without moving, afraid to disrupt the spell that had seemed to settle over the camp. He went on:

"We also knew of the prophecy that said a direct descendent of Tiernan would break Raelin's curse and reclaim the throne. But as talk of the prophecy increased, Raelin and Guthrie sent spies into the Colleland to find and kill Tiernan's descendents. It was because of these spies that my people began marking themselves on the left shoulder. The three-sided symbol was applied by a magic only known to a few in the Colleland, and that magic has been passed down by the Guardians of the Symbol ever since. It is a magic none can replicate, and it remains the way my people discern a friend from a spy."

Maddock looked down to the dirt. Some time passed before he spoke again:

"Despite the efforts of my people, however, over the years, spies managed to kill many who were discovered or just suspected to be from Tiernan's direct bloodline. Even my own parents were murdered."

It took a moment for Maddock's words to sink in, and then Edlyn stared at him, aghast. "Your parents were killed? Maddock, all my talk of my father's death must have brought you so much despair. I am sorry that I—"

"Why do you apologize?" Maddock peered at her. "I did not tell you, so how could you have known?"

Edlyn was taken aback that Maddock showed no emotion. He simply stared off into the night and kept speaking:

"I was thirteen when I came home and found my parents dead. From the wounds they had sustained, there was no question that the murders were committed by spies sent from Nereth."

Maddock stopped again, his eyes clouding over. Edlyn realized that, despite how he was trying to hide it, Maddock was harboring emotion, after all—terrible, gut-wrenching emotion that she understood all too well.

"Maddock, you do not need to speak more," Edlyn's own voice shook. "I did not realize that—"

"Edlyn, though profoundly difficult, his story should be told," Ailith counseled.

"No." Edlyn shook her head. "Maddock does not need to relive such horrible memories just because—"

"Edlyn, his story should be told," Ailith repeated with quiet urgency.

Edlyn glanced at Maddock again. He was somberly watching the fire, almost as if he had forgotten the others were there. Edlyn shrank back and hung her head, overwhelmed with guilt. After a while, she heard Maddock speak:

"Though I was orphaned, I was lucky. A friend of my father, a tailor named Ronan, offered me shelter and a chance to be his apprentice. So in addition to having learned my father's trade of metal working, I was given the opportunity to learn a second profession. It was quite an advantage in the little village where we lived."

Maddock's voice remained reassuringly even. Edlyn dared to fix her eyes on him once more.

"Ronan had no family of his own," Maddock was saying to no one. "I became like a son to him, and he was like an adoptive father to me. At times, though, Ronan would disappear from the village. When I finally asked Ronan why, he told me that he went to the mountains to develop other skills. As I got older, Ronan taught those skills to me. It was from him that I learned to use the sword and the dagger; and to fight, hunt, and truly use my senses."

"What became of Ronan?" Kegan inquired. "What happened to this good man who took you in?"

Maddock's tone changed, "Three months ago, when I turned eighteen, I knew it was time for me to find my own way in life. I said goodbye to Ronan and set out from our village. Where I intended to go, I knew not. I let my instincts guide me."

"You went alone, without a plan or destination," Edlyn remarked. "That was brave, Maddock."

"It was foolish," he corrected her with almost a smile, "yet I knew it was what I had to do."

A cold wind caused Edlyn to shift closer to the flames. Maddock watched her and then continued:

"Strangely, it was not toward the larger towns of the Colleland where I was drawn. Instead, I found myself heading to the Fierlen Mountains. Farther and farther I went, led by something that I did not understand. On the day I reached the summit, I saw a remarkable sight: inhabited lands far in the distance. Lands that no map had ever shown."

"Nereth," Edlyn whispered.

He nodded. "So it was here to Nereth that I was drawn, and it was here that I came. I entered the kingdom and gained employment in the first village I encountered, content to bide my time until I was prompted next to journey forth."

"Then, somehow, you went from employment to needing shelter in Ravenshire Forest," Kegan noted kindly.

"Yes," Maddock said. "One chilly morning, I found my employer's child—a disobedient, spoiled boy—trying to climb into the well. The boy fell, and I rescued him. But in the event, my shirt got torn. The symbol on my shoulder was revealed, and my employer discovered that I was from the Colleland."

"Your employer must have rejoiced to learn that someone from the Colleland was in Nereth," Edlyn declared. "What did he believe about the ancient prophecy?"

"Ancient prophecies do not matter to those who are desperate for reward money to pay ever-increasing taxes," Maddock cynically countered. "My employer informed Sheriff Hurst, and Sheriff Hurst reported me to the king and queen."

"Fear and treachery truly run deep if a person in Nereth is willing to betray one from the Colleland," Ailith noted solemnly.

Edlyn could not believe what she had heard. "What happened after they learned of you, Maddock?"

"The sheriff was swift to act," Maddock replied with resentment. "That very night, Sheriff Hurst, his deputy, and some of the king's soldiers stormed the barn where I slept. With swords drawn, they announced that they were on assignment to bring me to the king and queen. I fought, and it was during that fight when Sheriff Hurst dealt me the blow to my abdomen."

Edlyn cringed. "Had you not been so quick on your feet, that injury would have been fatal."

"Quickness was not enough," Maddock said. "I was outnumbered and trapped. I would have been captured had it not been for another who entered the fight: Ronan. I do not know how he found me, but Ronan came to my rescue that night. Together, we fought. More of our attackers fell. A pathway to escape opened. Ronan told me to run."

Maddock broke off. The others waited patiently—anxiously—until he talked again:

"I bolted from the barn and ran, believing Ronan was behind me. Only once I reached the foothills did I realize that I was alone. Staying in the shadows, I swiftly retraced my steps. When I approached the barn, I could see that Ronan was still fighting, keeping the attackers from following after me. But before I got close enough to rejoin him, Ronan surrendered. Ronan was taken away, and Sheriff Hurst and his company never knew that I was there." Maddock's eyes flashed fiercely. "That is why I remain in Nereth. I am here to rescue my adoptive father from the king and queen."

As quickly as it had come on, the fury in Maddock's eyes disappeared. He lowered his head. His story was done.

No one spoke for a long while.

"Maddock," Edlyn finally dared ask, "are you sure that Ronan is even still alive? Do you know whether this risk you take is worth it?"

He picked up a dry leaf and tossed it into the flames. "I do not know, but I am not going to leave Nereth until I have rescued Ronan or know that he is dead. If it is the latter, I will kill Sheriff Hurst, the king, and the queen myself."

"Those are vengeful words you speak. Be careful, Maddock, for the magic of the queen is strong," Ailith warned. "Raelin will sense your intentions and warn Guthrie of your plan."

"Raelin? Guthrie?" Edlyn peered in confusion at the Langerlan woman. "Ailith, you speak as if Raelin and Guthrie are alive still."

"Yes, Edlyn," Ailith replied. "Raelin and Guthrie reign over the Kingdom of Nereth to this day."

"That is impossible," Edlyn contended. "It has been centuries since they took the throne. They—"

"It is not impossible for a powerful sorceress," Kegan assured her. "Raelin's magic is stronger than any of us understand. She and her brother live on, undoubtedly due to a spell that she herself put upon them."

Edlyn was not convinced. "If that were so, we in Nereth would have known."

"How? Edlyn, have you ever seen the king or queen?" Ailith gently queried.

Edlyn responded cautiously, "No, but I am not the standard by which this can be judged. I lived my entire life on the manor and rarely strayed from it."

"Then you are the perfect standard," Ailith said. "Just like you, most in Nereth have never seen the king or queen. No one knows whose magic it is that continues bringing darkness upon this land."

"But we are speaking of *centuries*," Edlyn stated, still doubtful. "How could Raelin and Guthrie keep such a secret over all that time?"

"Undisguised, Raelin and Guthrie are in contact with only a small circle of their most trusted advisors, including the current sheriff, Sheriff Hurst," Ailith explained. "Otherwise, including those rare times when they travel beyond the castle, they are disguised by magic."

"Well, if they have such powerful, secretive magic, how can you be so sure that they live on?" Edlyn challenged.

"Ah, please allow me to explain," Kegan piped up. "You see, Ravenshire Forest parallels the river until it reaches the wall that surrounds the castle grounds. Through the centuries, from the relative safety of this forest, we Langerlen have kept a close watch over the comings and goings of those who cross the castle gates. In doing so, we have witnessed evidence of Raelin and Guthrie's continued existence. For example, a beggar woman once entered the forest, but as soon as she was hidden among the trees, that woman morphed into Raelin and gave instructions to Berax, who waited on her command. There have also been times over the centuries when Guthrie secretly traveled through here, bringing military instructions to his sheriff, unaware that we were observing." Kegan paused to smile at Edlyn and Maddock. "In fact, when the two of you first appeared in the forest, I followed because I wondered if Raelin and Guthrie were again among us. It did not take long, however, to realize that you were indeed as you appeared to be: a brave young woman and a stubborn, insightful young man."

Edlyn sat back, taking in all that she had been told. She then put a concerned eye on Maddock.

"Did you know that Raelin and Guthrie were still in power, and that they were the ones from whom you had sworn to rescue Ronan?"

"I did not know for sure, though I believed it to be so," Maddock answered, unaffected. "Like many in the Colleland, I suspected that Raelin and Guthrie continued to reign over the Kingdom of Nereth. There was no other way to explain the unrelenting presence of spies among my people. The way that the spies killed, the secrecy of their movements, their patterns unchanged for centuries—only Raelin's magic could be directing and protecting them still."

Edlyn stared at him, incredulous. "But what made you think that you could possibly rescue Ronan from them? You are up against evil and magic that no one understands."

"It does not matter what I am up against," Maddock responded.

Her mind filling with concerns too terrible to articulate, Edlyn exhaustedly dropped her head in her hands. But as fear and confusion further swelled inside of her, she raised her head again and put her eyes on the Langerlan.

"How do we know that you are not Raelin and Guthrie in disguise? How do we know that you are not here to encourage Maddock to pursue a mission that he will not live through?"

Maddock's eyebrows shot up. "Edlyn, the Langerlen—"

"We do not even know that they are real Langerlen, do we, Maddock?" Edlyn barely knew what she was saying anymore. "If Raelin has such magical powers, she and Guthrie could be in disguise and with us right now, could they not?"

Maddock took a breath and tried again, "Edlyn, they—"

"Edlyn, you are wise to wonder," Ailith told her, turning to Kegan.

Together, the Langerlen rolled up the left sleeves of their robes to reveal a symbol upon their shoulders—a symbol very similar to Maddock's

"That was what I was trying to tell you, Edlyn," Maddock said softly.

"The Man in White once visited Ravenshire Forest," Ailith explained to her. "He told us of the confusion that Raelin's spies were creating. Using magic only known to a few in the Colleland, the Man in White marked the Langerlen with a symbol of their own. That way, the true allies within the forest could always be identified."

With color rising in her cheeks, Edlyn shook her head. "I am sorry. You have both been so good to us. It was foolish of me to...I am tired and not thinking...please forgive me."

"There is nothing you need to ask forgiveness for," Ailith responded. "You are smart not to trust. You have entered the realm of evil magic, and it is good that you are skeptical. Continue to keep a sharp eye out, and be wary of all who claim to be your friend."

Edlyn met her gaze. Ailith smiled at her.

Kegan got to his feet. "It has grown very late, you are weary, and we should depart. This fire will burn sure and warm through the night. Sleep soundly, my friends."

The Langerlen stepped away from the fire, disappearing into the darkness. After a while, Maddock stood and extended his hand down to Edlyn. She did not take it.

"You are really going to try and enter Raelin and Guthrie's castle?" she asked, not quite able to look at him.

"Yes, Edlyn, I am."

"You might die."

"I might."

She stayed quiet. Maddock offered Edlyn his arm again. She let him put his hand around hers and help her to her feet.

"Then I am going to go with you," Edlyn informed him resolutely.

"You are not coming with me."

"You cannot stop me from—"

"As Kegan said, it has grown late," Maddock cut her off with a slight grin. "We should wait until morning when we are refreshed, and then we can continue this argument right where we left off."

Edlyn slowly began to smile.

Maddock let go of her hand. "Goodnight, Edlyn."

"Goodnight, Maddock."

7

The sound of a horse's gentle whinny caused Edlyn to open her eyes. At first, all was a blur. A recollection of a thousand strange events caused her to wonder what had been a dream and what was reality. But as her senses sharpened, Edlyn saw the tent roof above her and felt an earthen bed beneath her body. She then knew that everything had really happened, just as she remembered.

Edlyn pulled the blankets up under her chin. For the first time in years, she did not have to rush from a cot to tend animals, draw water from the well, chop wood, or prepare food. She had no floors to clean or clothes to wash. There were no threats of being beaten.

The life she had known was gone forever.

Edlyn pushed aside the blankets that had kept her warm through the night, sat up, and took deep breaths of the early morning air. Although it was barely growing light, she began hearing the sound of a horse already being saddled outside.

"Maddock?" she called softly.

Steady footsteps approached her tent and stopped near the door.

"How did you sleep, Edlyn?"

"Well," she answered, comforted by the sound of his voice. "And yourself?"

"My face was cold. I have decided that I do not like being cleanly shaven."

Edlyn laughed.

Maddock's tone became serious once again, "Now as soon as you are ready, we must be off. It will not be long before Sheriff Hurst and the king's soldiers resume their search for us. We need to move quickly."

"Of course. I shall make haste."

As Maddock walked away, Edlyn jumped up, put on a cloak, and swiftly braided her long hair. She next bent down to roll up her blankets but stopped abruptly. Reaching under the collar of her dress, she discovered that her necklace was gone. Edlyn let out a cry.

Maddock ran back to the tent and threw its door open, dagger in hand. He swiftly scanned the scene and then peered at her. "What is the matter?"

"My necklace is gone! I had it on when I went to sleep last night, and now—"

"Necklace?" Maddock stepped inside, putting his dagger away. "What necklace?"

"It was my mother's!" Edlyn dropped to her knees and frantically searched the bedding. "I cannot lose it, Maddock!"

Maddock crouched beside her. "Did it come off while you were sleeping?"

"I do not know!"

Edlyn continued throwing blankets aside while Maddock got up to inspect the rest of the tent. To her dismay, the necklace was nowhere to be found. As tears began rolling down her cheeks, Edlyn heard Maddock speak:

"Edlyn."

She kept her eyes down. "I know, Maddock. We must go, and I cannot delay any longer."

"Edlyn," he said again.

She looked at him. Maddock was pointing behind her. Edlyn whipped around and let out a new cry, this time one of relief. In the dirt, something shimmered in the morning light. Edlyn reached out with shaking hands and lifted the necklace, watching the triangle-shaped medallion sparkle, and then she clutched the treasure to her chest and suppressed a sob of relief.

"We must go," Maddock said again. "I will finish getting the horses ready."

Still facing away from him, Edlyn nodded. Once Maddock stepped out again into the growing daylight, Edlyn brushed her tears away, carefully put on the necklace, and gathered her bedding. Clutching her things, she walked outside. She quickly stopped in disbelief.

With the exception of her tent, all evidence of their camp was gone. Kegan's fire had burned away, and the stones from which it had been generated sat unimportantly on the dirt. The supplies were already packed and strapped over the horses' backs. Even the marks of the Berax attack were no longer seen.

"You should have woken me. I could have helped, Maddock," Edlyn chastised. "You did not need to do this all yourself."

Maddock strode toward her. "There was a time you let me rest when I needed it most. I was only doing the same."

He passed Edlyn and began dismantling her tent. Edlyn quickly tossed her bag over Cynric's back and returned to help.

"Where are we going to go from here?" she asked as they worked.

"We are going to get you somewhere safe," Maddock replied, cinching the rest of their belongings to the horses. "After that, I will continue on my journey to rescue Ronan."

Edlyn made herself remain calm. "Maddock, as we discussed, I am not going to let you abandon me somewhere, and I am certainly not going to let you attempt to enter the castle alone."

He swung up onto Zanavian and motioned to the sky. "We had better get going. It is about to rain."

"Ignoring me will not change things." Edlyn mounted Cynric and took the reins. "Try as you might, you are not going to make me angry, either."

He tipped his head. "That is unfortunate. I like the way your eyes flash when you are angry."

With a grin, Maddock nudged Zanavian to get underway. Edlyn shook her head and urged Cynric to follow.

As Maddock predicted, drops of rain began falling, and the forest soon filled with the sound of water pattering upon the foliage. Edlyn pulled the hood of her cloak up over her head, shivering as the cold soaked through her clothes and chilled her skin. They continued riding in silence until, without warning, Maddock pulled Zanavian to a halt and grabbed his dagger.

"Maddock?" Edlyn exclaimed. "What is—"

"Shh," he whispered. "Someone is following."

Edlyn tugged on Cynric's reins and reached for her sword. She listened carefully but heard nothing except for the rain.

"Fugitive, you are in danger," a voice said.

Edlyn checked behind her. As if materializing from the air, Kegan appeared before them.

"What news?" Maddock asked, putting his dagger away.

"Sheriff Hurst and the soldiers have left the castle. Some are heading for the river, and the rest are moving to surround the forest," Kegan told them. "None are breaking off to search elsewhere. They must be certain you are here."

"How?" Edlyn demanded as the frigid rain started pouring down harder. "How could the sheriff have discovered our whereabouts?"

"I am sure that the sheriff discovered nothing on his own. He can be no more certain of your location than any other mortal," Kegan replied. "But Raelin's powers are strong; you were getting close, and she must have sensed the danger."

Maddock glanced off into the distance and then focused again on the Langerlan. "How much time do we have, Kegan?"

"They exited the castle gates at first light."

While a loud rumble of thunder rolled through the sky, Maddock's jaw clenched worriedly.

"What is wrong?" Edlyn pressed. "What is it, Maddock?"

Maddock faced her. "With soldiers surrounding the forest, we have no choice but to cross the river to escape. We need to get to the water before the other soldiers make it there."

"Then let us be off." Edlyn turned Cynric in the direction of the river. "We—"

"No," Maddock interrupted. "No horses."

Edlyn stopped, unsure if she had heard him correctly. "What?"

"The terrain on the eastern side of the river is treacherous, and the horses would only slow us down. Our journey from here must be on foot."

"But we cannot leave them," Edlyn protested, placing a protective hand upon Cynric's neck.

"They will be safe. We will keep them in the forest under our care," Kegan assured her. "Now grab your weapons and go, friends. You must flee without delay."

Maddock dismounted Zanavian and unstrapped his things. Edlyn reluctantly slid off of Cynric's back, reached out, and stroked the horse's nose.

"Farewell, dear Cynric," she whispered while the horse gave her an affectionate nudge.

"Hurry, Kegan. Take the animals and hide," Maddock instructed him over the growing storm. "Short of capturing one from the Colleland, I am sure there is nothing more Sheriff Hurst would like than to imprison a Langerlan."

Kegan took the horses by the reins. "Travel safely, my friends."

"Thank you," Edlyn called, but Kegan and the animals had already disappeared. Edlyn gazed after them, the rain chilling her body and a painful ache filling her heart.

"Come, Edlyn," Maddock insisted. "We must move."

Maddock began running eastward for the river, dagger in hand and sword at his side. Edlyn took a deep breath and charged after him. Wiping the rain from her face, she pushed through the branches, squinting to see where Maddock had gone. Suddenly, a strong hand gripped her by the wrist and yanked her down to the rain-soaked earth.

"Stay low," Maddock told Edlyn in her ear before she could let out a yell of surprise.

Crouched in the bushes, Maddock and Edlyn peered out from the trees. Just beyond the forest's edge, they could see the wide river rolling past, its water gray and foaming, churning angrily in the storm. On the opposite side of the river, the steep eastern bank rose up until it became hidden by low, misty clouds.

Edlyn turned to Maddock, not hiding her concern. "You cannot swim, and these swords will weigh us down. How are we going to cross without—"

"We are too late," Maddock growled. "There are already soldiers on the other side."

Heart pounding with fear, Edlyn checked again through the trees. On the far side of the river, soldiers were hiking down to the water's edge, moving unsteadily over the rocky, slippery terrain. When a flash of lightning lit the sky, Edlyn clapped a hand over her mouth to muffle her own gasp. Sheriff Hurst was leading them.

"At least they will not cross back to this side of the river from there," Maddock stated, studying the soldiers' movements. "The current is too swift and the water too deep."

Edlyn wiped rain from her face. "Then what are they doing over there?"

"Waiting to catch us if we attempt to cross," Maddock answered, still watching the enemies that lined the opposite shore. Brushing the wet hair from his eyes, he peered downriver. "There is only one way those soldiers could have made it from the castle to the eastern side of the river. There must be a bridge farther to the south."

Edlyn's heart was racing. "Then we should stay hidden in the forest, go farther south to find that bridge ourselves, and try to cross without being seen."

"It is our only chance, and we must do so before we become surrounded."

Motioning for Edlyn to stay down, Maddock backed up farther into the cover of the trees. After another glance out at the soldiers, Maddock nodded to her. Edlyn took her cue, silently retreating until she had reached Maddock's side. Concealed again within the woods, they resumed racing south as fast as their feet would take them. An icy wind blew, causing the stinging rain to fly sideways and obscure their sight.

Thunder rumbled overhead, and the sky grew even darker.

Suddenly, a pair of glowing, yellow eyes appeared in front of them.

"Berax! Get down!" Maddock yelled above the wind.

Edlyn threw herself forward onto the drenched dirt. She heard a terrifying growl as the beast leapt over her. Maddock grasped Edlyn and pulled her back to her feet, placing himself between Edlyn and the monster. The beast started to pace in front of them, snarling and baring its teeth. Maddock raised his dagger. Edlyn stepped to Maddock's side and lifted her sword. The animal turned toward her and narrowed its eyes, looking at her necklace. For one moment, Edlyn and the beast stared at each other. Then it sprang.

Maddock leapt in front of Edlyn, thrusting his dagger into the beast's abdomen. The Berax let out a shriek.

"Strike, Edlyn!" Maddock cried. "Strike now!"

Edlyn rushed the animal, sword raised. But the wounded beast scampered away before she could make her blow. While the rain fell harder, Edlyn shakily sheathed her weapon. With another uncertain look at where the Berax had fled, she took off her necklace. Using her wet, cold hands, Edlyn placed the necklace inside a small pocket that was buried within the folds her dress, and she drew the pocket's drawstring tight.

"The Berax will tell the king of our location!" Maddock had to shout to be heard over the storm. "We must get to the bridge! Hurry!"

Lightning flashed when Edlyn and Maddock started running once more. The rain turned to sleet, causing the uneven ground to become dangerously slick and forcing them to slow their pace. Eventually, Maddock raised an arm, motioned to their left, and sprinted that way. Edlyn bolted after him. The forest thinned again. Just before reaching the edge of the woods, Maddock once more held out his arm. They both came to a halt.

Catching her breath, Edlyn watched through the trees as the swollen river coursed ominously past. She shot another concerned glance at Maddock but found that the water was not what had his attention. He was looking downriver, focused on something else. Shifting to see what Maddock was staring at, Edlyn instantly felt a petrifying sensation stir within her. Far in the distance, on their side of the river, stood the castle of King Guthrie and Queen Raelin, its sharp peaks and towers rising toward the sky, surrounded by thick storm clouds.

It was a long time before Maddock pulled his eyes away from the castle. He pointed downriver. "There it is."

Shivering, Edlyn squinted to see through the storm. She could barely discern the outline of a bridge stretching across the river to the eastern shore. Edlyn grew increasingly apprehensive, observing how the water splashed against the bridge and swirled furiously underneath.

"Sheriff Hurst and the soldiers with him are not guarding the bridge," she heard Maddock note suspiciously. "That makes no sense, unless..."

"Unless?" Edlyn echoed with unease. "Unelss what?"

"Unless the soldiers who remained on this side of the river are coming." He reached for his dagger and turned around, facing the forest.

Over the storm, Edlyn began hearing shouts and barking dogs. Pulse racing, she put her hand upon her sword and also spun to face the trees. As the commotion grew louder, Edlyn shuddered. The soldiers were charging though the forest, headed right for them.

"There will be too many to fight! We must run, Edlyn!" Maddock shouted. "Run for the bridge and—"

He was cut off when a familiar sound rang through the forest. Soldiers' cries of surprise and pain were heard, and as lightning flashed, Edlyn and Maddock could see the silhouettes of the soldiers who were being thrust into the air by an invisible power.

"Langerlen!" Edlyn exclaimed with relief.

She and Maddock looked in the direction from which the sound had come. Standing among the trees, Ailith, Kegan, and other Langerlen were each holding a glass sphere in their hands.

"Go now," Ailith commanded them. "Get to the bridge."

A deafening clap of thunder shook the ground as Edlyn and Maddock bolted from the forest and sprinted for the bridge. Edlyn again heard the mysterious sound followed by more soldiers' shrieks, but she did not look back. Lungs burning in the frigid air, she kept racing alongside Maddock down the muddy riverbank. As another bolt of lightning lit the sky, they reached the narrow staircase at the base of the bridge.

Gripping the wet handrails of the staircase, Edlyn began to climb. Maddock followed. Up the slippery, uneven steps they rose until the cracked, gaping wooden planks of the bridge were before them, stretching over the river to the opposite shore. From her vantage point, Edlyn took the chance to check over her shoulder. Despite the Langerlen's attack, soldiers were beginning to emerge from the forest and run down the riverbank.

"They are coming!" Edlyn shouted to Maddock.

Maddock pushed past her. Holding tightly to the side of the bridge, he stepped onto the first few boards that were precariously suspended over the water. He then held out a hand for Edlyn.

"It is stable. We can cross safely. Hurry!"

Edlyn ventured after him, and they began inching forward together. Swells of icy water struck, and the bridge swayed violently under their feet. Relentlessly, another wave hit, forcing Edlyn to wait and hold on until the shaking subsided. When the wave cleared, Edlyn caught another glimpse behind them.

"Maddock, the soldiers are almost at the bridge!" she screamed, her voice barely audible above the storm.

Maddock did not respond. He was standing stiffly, looking at something in front of them.

"What is wrong?" Edlyn called out, clinging to the railing to keep from toppling over.

If he answered, she did not hear him. Edlyn leaned forward to see what had caused Maddock to ready his dagger. Through the downpour, she saw Sheriff Hurst and his group of soldiers at the far end of the bridge, blocking their escape to the eastern shore.

Maddock reached an arm back for Edlyn, and they began a cautious retreat. Sheriff Hurst said something to his men before he started to advance across the bridge alone, his movements hesitant as he moved upon its slick, swaying surface.

There was a round of shouts from the other riverbank. Looking over her shoulder, Edlyn saw that the soldiers from the forest had reached the western side of the bridge. Gathered at the base of the steps, the soldiers were waiting with weapons drawn. Edlyn and Maddock were trapped.

"Edlyn, surrender!" Maddock shouted.

"What?" she yelled back.

More thunder rattled the sky as Maddock faced her. "Surrender! The sheriff will not let them hurt you! It is the only way you will be safe!"

Another wave rose over the side of the bridge and dropped down on top of them. Edlyn reached out to support herself as the bridge rocked from the impact. When the water cleared, Edlyn could see Sheriff Hurst. He had resumed his approach, looking directly at her with a triumphant smile on his face.

"Edlyn, surrender!" Maddock repeated over the roar of the wind.

"No!" she cried. "I will not—"

There was a flash of lightning and a boom of thunder directly overhead, followed by a crack and an enormous splash. The soldiers on both riverbanks began shouting frantically and pointing upriver. Behind Maddock, Edlyn saw Sheriff Hurst raise his head and peer out at the water. His malicious expression became one of terror, and he started moving as fast as he could back to the eastern shore.

Edlyn and Maddock turned to see what was causing the commotion. A huge tree, split by the lightning strike, had fallen into the water and was careening rapidly down the river—headed directly for the bridge.

Maddock put a strong arm around Edlyn's waist. "Edlyn, take off your sword and hang on!"

They were the last words she heard Maddock say. Edlyn had only enough time to yank the heavy sword from her body before the massive tree crashed into the bridge. The air filled with the sound of splintering wood. Torn from its anchoring posts, the bridge lurched and tipped. Edlyn was thrown to her knees as the wooden planks beneath her gave way. For a single moment, she seemed to hover in the air. Then she plummeted downward.

An instant later, Edlyn smacked into the icy water. Her head became submerged, and the noise of the storm turned to silence. She flailed in the ghostlike quiet as broken pieces from the bridge rammed into her body. Edlyn righted herself and attempted to swim for the surface, but her cloak was caught on a broken piece of wood. With her body screaming for air, Edlyn fought to free herself from the cloak, which twisted around her face and arms. Just when she could hold her breath no longer, she managed to grab the cloak's clasp at her neck and make a desperate pull. The cloak fell away. Her body began to rise.

Edlyn's head emerged above water. She gasped for breath while the stinging rain hit her face and the overwhelming noise of the storm again filled her ears. She was moving uncontrollably downriver, tossed by the swell and knocked by wreckage of the bridge that swirled past. She could see nothing but waves and rain.

"Maddock!" she screamed.

She had only enough time to take another breath before her body was thrust underwater once more. The next moment, she was pushed sickeningly upward. As the river coursed farther south, Edlyn continued to be thrown mercilessly about. When she was lifted up on another wave, she spotted Maddock, face down in the water.

Edlyn was dunked under the surface again. She paddled, fighting to steer her body toward where Maddock was last seen. She rose on a wave, only to be thrown under by another. Edlyn flailed until her arm hit against something. It was Maddock, submerged and dropping. Edlyn reached but could not get a grip on him before she was pushed upward by the current. Struggling against the force of the water, she dove. Her hand found Maddock's wrist, and she wrapped an arm around his waist. Clenching him tightly, she kicked to the surface.

"Hang on, Maddock!" she cried when their heads popped out of the water.

Up and down they rose and fell together while being pulled along by the river. As they rounded another bend, Edlyn spotted a low tree branch that was hanging over the water. Reaching out with one arm, Edlyn managed to get her numb fingers around the branch and hold on, despite the powerful momentum of the river that tried to yank her onward. Summoning all of her remaining strength, Edlyn tugged on the branch, pulling Maddock and herself toward the riverbank. When her feet scraped the river bottom, Edlyn let go of the branch, put both arms around Maddock's chest, and dragged him to shore. She set him flat on the ground. He did not move. Edlyn collapsed to her knees and pushed hard on his abdomen.

"Breathe, Maddock!"

She pumped again. And again. Under her hands, she felt his body lurch. He curled up and began coughing up water. Edlyn rolled him onto his side until his coughing ceased, and then she positioned Maddock again on his back.

"Maddock, can you hear me?" she shouted.

His blue lips trembled slightly, but he did not respond.

Edlyn shook him by the shoulders. "Maddock! Answer me!"

His eyelids flickered and opened. At first, there was no awareness behind his glassy, dark eyes. But slowly, life began to return to his face. He focused on her.

"I think you need to teach me how to swim," he remarked, his voice hoarse and weak.

Edlyn let out an exhausted, relieved cry and collapsed onto the mud beside him. Only then did she notice that the torrential rain had ceased. While the storm continued to calm, the two of them remained where they were for a long time. Finally, Edlyn heard Maddock speak:

"We have no supplies, no horses, and no food."

She turned her head toward him. "This is true."

"The only weapon that we have left is my dagger," he went on, still breathing hard as he stared up at the clouded sky.

"Yes."

"We are drenched and nearly frozen, and we are lost somewhere on the eastern side of the river."

"Correct."

"The king's best soldiers are hunting us."

"I believe you are right."

There was a pause.

"This is not exactly the way that I intended for our day to go," he noted.

Edlyn stared at him and then actually began to laugh. Maddock smiled, but for only a moment. As his expression became serious once again, Edlyn's laughter died away.

"Edlyn, I am sorry," he told her.

She sat up and rubbed her ice-cold hands together. "You have no reason to apologize, Maddock. I chose to join you on this journey."

He also sat up and then pushed a strand of her drenched hair from her face. "But you deserve better than this, Edlyn. Much better."

Edlyn could only gaze back at him, silenced by the intense, confused feelings that were rushing into her heart.

Maddock got to his feet. "Come. It is too cold out here. We must find shelter."

8

"We will soon be high enough to have a good view of the valley," Maddock called over his shoulder.

Behind him, Edlyn slipped on some loose rocks and fell forward, clumsily putting out her arms to catch herself. "V...very good," she stuttered.

As Maddock moved on, Edlyn did her best to climb after him. But her pace had slowed significantly in the hours since they had started scaling the hills that rose up from the eastern side of the river, and Edlyn was finding it increasingly difficult to keep up.

"I see a ledge," Maddock announced, rapidly outdistancing her. "I will go see what is visible from there."

Maddock picked up his speed and was soon lost from Edlyn's view. Meanwhile, Edlyn was forced to stop, seized with a coughing fit. When she finally caught her breath, she pressed forward, the still-damp clothing that hung on her body growing ever more frigid underneath the clouded sky. She clenched her fists in a feeble attempt to warm them, though her hands had long since lost their feeling.

"Edlyn?" Maddock asked from beyond where she could see.

Edlyn could not respond. It was taking all her energy just to focus on moving one leg in front of the other. Even her shivering had quieted into a steady, dull ache that saturated her entire core.

"Edlyn?" Maddock repeated.

"I am c...coming," she forced herself to say, blinking to get her vision to focus.

Trudging past a grouping of large boulders, Edlyn found Maddock standing on a rocky ledge that overlooked the valley below. When she went to Maddock's side, she was met by an incredible sight.

It seemed as though the entire Kingdom of Nereth stretched out before them. Far below, the wide river wound through the green valley until it disappeared into the horizon. Back on the west side of the river, the castle remained surrounded by storm clouds and thick fog. Adjacent to the castle and paralleling the river was Ravenshire Forest, dark and mysteriously still. Far beyond the forest, small villages and farmlands dotted the countryside.

"I see no soldiers," Maddock remarked, his eyes continuing to scan below. "They must have returned to the castle."

Edlyn's teeth chattered. "Wh...what about Sheriff Hurst and th...those with him on this side of the river?"

"No doubt they are also warm and comfortable within the castle walls," Maddock commented, still looking about. "Whether by boat, another bridge, or some other means, I am certain that Sheriff Hurst got himself safely back to shelter."

"Y...yes," Edlyn replied.

"But the fact that the sheriff and his soldiers are gone bodes well for us, Edlyn," Maddock added. "If he thought we had survived, the sheriff would have kept some soldiers out to search for us. Sheriff Hurst must assume us dead, which is obviously to our advantage."

Edlyn could only nod.

Maddock turned to his left. "This eastern side of the river does not appear to be uninhabited, after all. There are a few dwellings remaining in these hills."

Edlyn shifted to see what he was pointing at, having to catch herself when she swayed. Once she got her footing, she spotted the few small homes and farms that were many miles off.

Maddock tipped his head back and checked farther up the hillside. "There are old hunting caves about an hour's hike up from here. We will be able to find protection and light a fire without being visible."

He hurried off. Edlyn realized that he was still speaking to her, but she could not comprehend anything he was saying anymore. When she tried to move away from the ledge to go after him, her body would not react. A frigid wind blew as Edlyn stood senseless on the edge of the cliff.

"Edlyn!"

Maddock's voice was sharp and loud in her ear, as if he once more stood beside her. Edlyn then felt his hands grip hers. Slowly, she put her eyes on him. Through hazy vision, she saw that Maddock appeared extremely alarmed.

"Wh...what?" Edlyn stammered. "What is w...wrong?"

Observing Edlyn closely for the first time in hours, Maddock's expression grew panicked. He threw his arm around her and began leading her from the edge. "Edlyn, your skin is like ice. How long have you been like this? Why did you not tell me?"

"I...cold...nothing we could...in the river..."

As Edlyn deliriously fell quiet, Maddock guided her to a level area of ground, which was shielded from the wind by a boulder. He carefully sat her down and began trying to warm her hands with his. Lightheaded, Edlyn swayed and tipped. Maddock reached out to support her.

"Stay with me, Edlyn. Do you hear? You stay with me."

Edlyn did not reply. Her body was becoming limp, and her thoughts were blurred. Maddock leapt to his feet and backed away, and Edlyn realized that he was preparing to start a fire.

"Not...not here," she mumbled. "Too bright...they will see."

"It does not matter. You must get warm."

Edlyn swallowed past her swollen throat and pushed herself to her feet. "K...keep going. We...will find...somewhere."

She attempted to take a step. Her head spun, and she nearly fell. Maddock sprang forward and grabbed hold of her.

"Edlyn, you must..."

Edlyn could no longer hear him. She sensed her heart make a few slow thumps in her chest, and then her vision dimmed. Her legs gave out. Maddock lifted her in his arms.

"Do not leave me Edlyn," he whispered in her ear.

Then he began to walk.

***

Edlyn opened her eyes. Her head was against Maddock's chest, and she could feel the steady, rocking motion of his rapid footsteps as he carried her.

"M...Maddock."

He looked down at her, his face lined and anxious. "I am taking you to one of the farm homes in these eastern hills. We are not far now."

"But what if...they tell the sheriff?"

"It is a risk we have to take."

Edlyn's body ached, and her head swirled. She could stay awake no longer. As thunder rumbled through the sky, her awareness faded and her head fell back once more.

***

"You seek shelter."

"Yes. Please. For her. I will go elsewhere."

"You are not from here, young man."

Edlyn moaned and attempted to open her eyes when she heard an elderly woman speak, but she could not. Only half-conscious, Edlyn realized that she was still draped in Maddock's arms. Rain was falling upon her face. Her head was throbbing, and her skin was feverish. Her throat had grown sore and almost too tight to swallow.

"Please," was Maddock's strained request. "I fear that we do not have much time."

There was silence. Edlyn felt a wrinkled hand touch her forehead. Although small and frail, there was wisdom in the old woman's touch.

"Bring her inside," the woman said.

Edlyn felt Maddock carry her forward. A door was closed behind them, and the cold and wind were suddenly replaced by warmth and the sound of a crackling fire. Edlyn's nose filled with the aromas of meat and vegetables simmering somewhere nearby. Maddock's footsteps quickly crossed over a wooden floor, and Edlyn heard another door being pushed ajar. Maddock walked a few steps more and then bent down. Edlyn sensed herself being placed upon a soft bed.

"You are exhausted yourself, young man," the old woman remarked, peeling off Edlyn's drenched shoes and socks.

"I am fine," Maddock stated, sounding as though he was already moving away. "I will be back tomorrow to check on—"

"There is stew on the fire. Go have some supper."

"I do not want to intrude upon your kindness."

"You are intruding upon no one, young man," the old woman replied. "You are my guest now, just as she is, and I am not about to send you back into that storm."

"I truly did not intend—"

"Hush. No more protests. I am honored to have you both under my roof, for only something very important could have brought you two up into these hills. And only one with a noble heart would have carried her so far in a storm such as this. I insist that you eat and rest."

There was a pause. Edlyn then heard a door creak on its hinges and close softly. Maddock's footsteps faded. In the quiet that followed, there was the sound of the old woman walking away from the bed, followed by a scraping noise. Edlyn began to sense the heat of a stoked fire.

"I must get you warmed up, my dear," Edlyn heard the woman tell her.

Edlyn tossed her head. "Necklace...pocket."

The old woman did not reply as she stripped Edlyn's freezing clothes off of her body. Hot stones were placed on the bed, and a blanket was laid over her. Edlyn let out an agonized groan as the intense heat caused deep, searing discomfort to course through her.

"Try to relax, my dear," the old woman said, brushing Edlyn's forehead soothingly.

The overpowering discomfort in Edlyn's body evolved into a strange sensation of both ice and fire. Edlyn let out a cry as her skin began to prickle and sting. Then she felt warmth. She breathed slowly and became still. The old woman reached out and palpated Edlyn's wrist for a few seconds and then let go.

"Your heart is awakening, my dear."

Edlyn gradually opened her eyes. She found herself in a small room that felt cozy and welcoming despite its sparse furnishings. Through a window on her left, Edlyn could see the dark storm raging outside. Light and warmth came from a flickering fireplace to her right. Edlyn lastly turned her head to focus on the person who was seated beside the bed.

The old woman was willowy, with stringy white hair that hung past her shoulders. Her skin was weather-worn and wrinkled, but her light eyes were alert and sharp. She wore a simple dress with a shawl draped over her shoulders.

"Hello, dear," the woman greeted her.

"Neck...lace," was all Edlyn replied, her voice hoarse.

The old woman leaned toward her. "What is your name, dear?"

"Ed...lyn."

"My name is Vanora."

Edlyn shivered feverishly while her eyes scanned the room. "My neck...my necklace."

Vanora followed Edlyn's agitated gaze. The woman stood up and walked to the other side of the room, where Edlyn's wet dress hung over a chair near the fire.

"Is what you seek in here?"

"Y...yes."

Vanora came back to the bed with the dress in hand. Edlyn attempted to sit up, but her aching head began to spin. She collapsed back onto the pillow.

Vanora sat down beside her once more. "I see that I shall not get you to rest until we find what it is that you are so worried about."

Edlyn watched uneasily as Vanora used her hands to pat around the skirt of the wet gown. Finally,

Vanora paused as though she had felt something. She pressed her hands onto the skirt again.

"Ah, there is something in this pocket," the woman remarked.

Edlyn forced herself to keep her eyes open as Vanora found the pocket and unloosed the drawstring that kept it closed.

"Now, now, here it is," Vanora said reassuringly, pulling the necklace out. "You can rest soundly, knowing that..." Vanora went quiet when her eyes fell upon the emblem that hung on the chain. She fixed her curious attention on Edlyn once more. "This is yours?"

Edlyn only looked back at her, too exhausted to reply.

Vanora carefully draped the necklace over Edlyn's head. "Rest now," the woman told her. "I will be back to see you soon."

Edlyn watched Vanora step away from the bed and hang her dress back up to dry. With a last check over her shoulder, Vanora exited the room and closed the door. Alone in the stillness, Edlyn listened to the fire, which burned comfortingly close by. Edlyn's eyes began to droop. Then she dropped into a deep sleep.

***

"I have brought in extra firewood. The storm continues to swell outside," someone stated.

Vanora replied, "Thank you, Peyton."

There was a pause.

"So this is the young woman," the person named Peyton said, sounding as if he had come closer to the bed.

Edlyn began to stir when she heard the unfamiliar man's voice. It was gruff but not unfriendly.

"Yes," Vanora answered.

"Where is her companion?"

"Resting," Vanora replied. "He spent all night sitting outside her room. Only once the morning came did he finally agree to sleep."

"Did they say anything about what brought them here?"

"The young man, Maddock, has said nothing. I sense that he is harboring great secrets."

"And her?" Peyton inquired.

"She mumbled things throughout the night but nothing of sense."

Vanora approached the bed and took hold of Edlyn's wrist. Edlyn shifted and awoke. The woman was leaning over her, monitoring her pulse. Behind her stood a broad-chested man who appeared a few years older than Edlyn. He had dark blond hair and a short beard. An axe hung at his side. He was observing Edlyn with eyes that were just like Vanora's. When the man realized that Edlyn was watching him, he abruptly averted his gaze and moved for the door.

"Th...thank you," Edlyn called after him.

It seemed to take a moment before Peyton realized that Edlyn had addressed him. He stopped in the doorway, turned, and peered back at her.

"For the w...wood," Edlyn added, her strength nearly gone.

Peyton made a stiff bow and then left the room.

"That is my son, Peyton," Vanora explained to Edlyn once he had gone. "He lives with me here."

Edlyn wearily rested her head back. She realized that she was in a clean change of clothes, and her long hair had been washed and combed.

"I have breakfast for you," Vanora stated, bringing a bowl over to her.

Edlyn's stomach churned uncomfortably. "Th...thank you, but I...am not hungry."

"You have to try, Edlyn. It is important."

"I...cannot."

Vanora set the bowl down, reached out, and rested her hand again on Edlyn's forehead. An expression of concern passed over the woman's face. Edlyn noticed nothing else before she drifted off to sleep.

***

Edlyn felt someone's steady hands lift her head.

"Edlyn, you must drink."

It was Maddock. Edlyn made a sound and opened her eyes. She saw him seated on the edge of her bed, holding her up. Beside him, Vanora gripped a wooden cup, which she placed against Edlyn's lips. Edlyn forced herself to take a sip.

"That is better," Maddock told her, but although he put a smile on his face, he appeared exhausted and worried.

"You...have not slept much," Edlyn observed.

Maddock said nothing.

"Take some more, my dear," Vanora instructed and raised the cup again.

As Edlyn dipped her head and drank, the door to the room was opened. Peyton stepped inside, covered in mud and drenched with rain. He was holding a small bag. He paused when he noticed Maddock and then turned to Vanora.

"The herbs," Peyton announced, holding the bag up.

Maddock had stopped at the intrusion and looked over his shoulder. Peyton handed the bag to his mother and then met Maddock's stare. Neither of the young men spoke.

"Maddock, this is my son, Peyton," Vanora explained. She gestured between them. "Peyton, this is our other guest, Maddock."

Maddock nodded stiffly. "We thank you for giving us shelter here, Peyton."

"It was my mother who took you in, not me." Peyton shifted his focus to Edlyn, his stern expression unchanged. "You are awake."

"And you...are wet," Edlyn replied.

The harsh look on Peyton's face faltered slightly.

"Is this all, Peyton?" Vanora asked, reaching into the bag.

Pulling his attention from Edlyn, Peyton nodded to his mother. "I searched the entire hillside. Everything else was destroyed by the storm."

Appearing greatly troubled, Vanora addressed the two young men, "I must mix this medicine immediately. Stay with her until she has had the rest of that potion."

Vanora handed Maddock the cup before hurrying away with the bag. As the door shut behind her, there was a strained quiet. Peyton stepped to the fire, placed a new log onto the flames, and watched it burn. Maddock faced Edlyn and held the potion out to her.

Edlyn resisted. "I do not...think that I can take more."

Maddock did not relent. "You have to try."

Peyton muttered something and headed for the door, his strong, heavy footsteps causing the wooden floorboards to creak beneath his boots. But when he reached for the latch, Peyton looked back.

"Why have you come here, Maddock?"

Maddock carefully rested Edlyn onto her pillow, put the cup aside, and faced Peyton directly. "I cannot tell you."

Peyton gestured to Edlyn. "Is it worth killing her over? For that is what you nearly did."

Maddock swiftly got to his feet. "Do not lecture me about things that you do not understand."

"Maddock...stop." Edlyn tried to sit up. "Peyton is...helping us."

Maddock clenched his jaw but stayed silent.

"What about my mother?" Peyton went on. "Or me? Have you put us in danger by asking us to harbor you here?"

Maddock's eyes drifted to the window. "I do not know, Peyton," he replied.

They were interrupted when the bedroom door was opened. Vanora entered hurriedly, holding a vile filled with dark liquid. She halted abruptly when she observed the scene.

"What is this about?" the old woman asked the two young men, though from her tone she seemed to already know the answer.

Neither Maddock nor Peyton replied.

With a shake of her head, Vanora approached Edlyn's bed. "Here, my dear, you must drink this," Vanora told her gently. Once Edlyn began to sip, Vanora shifted so that she again faced the others. She spoke to them sharply, "Gentlemen, there are far bigger issues at present than what you bicker over—issues that profoundly affect us all. So I will not tolerate any petty nonsense between the two of you. Is that clear?"

Without a word, Peyton walked out of the room. They could hear his boots crossing the main part of the house, followed by the sound of the front door being opened and then closed again with a slam.

"Forgive him, Maddock," Vanora said. "Ever since his father died, he worries too much about my safety."

Maddock also remained silent, his eyes shifting from Vanora to the direction in which Peyton had gone.

Vanora helped Edlyn finish her medicine and settle in bed. While Edlyn started drifting off to sleep, Vanora once again put her attention on Maddock.

"What is on your mind, young man?"

"I must depart from this place before harm comes to anyone."

"No!" Edlyn deliriously cried out, struggling to get up. "Do not leave...me here! I...am going with you!"

Vanora reached out and held Edlyn by the shoulders. "Hush, dear. Hush."

Edlyn collapsed onto her pillow, breathing hard and stirring restlessly.

"No one is going to leave," Vanora went on, whispering in Edlyn's ear and brushing her hair until Edlyn's moaning quieted. The old lady then stood and walked to Maddock's side. "No more talk like that. Edlyn is not yet strong, and she needs you here. If you were to leave now, it would be a blow that I do not think she would recover from."

Maddock flinched and stared down at Edlyn, eyes wide.

"I think that you need her, too," Vanora added, observing him in the firelight. "More than you even realize."

Maddock shook his head. "I meant to journey alone. I never intended to put anyone in danger."

"Yes, but whether we intend it or not, sometimes our path crosses that of others, nonetheless," Vanora noted wisely. "Although we may not be able to see it at the time, those crossings—which may or may not be due to chance—are for our good."

9

A loud pounding caused Edlyn to awaken with a start. It was nighttime, and the only light came from the fire that burned in the bedroom fireplace. Edlyn had no idea how long she had been asleep. She heard the pounding again, which seemed to be coming from the front door. Disoriented, Edlyn pushed the blankets off of her, sat up unsteadily, and weakly swung her legs out of bed. The startling, repetitive banging disturbed the stillness once more.

"Open up in the name of the king!" came an angry shout.

Edlyn's body seized with fear. She stood up as fast as she could, nearly letting out a scream when the door to her bedroom was thrown open.

"Edlyn, make no sound," Maddock whispered. He ran forward and lifted her in his arms. "The king's soldiers are outside."

More footsteps rapidly approached the bedroom. Maddock spun toward the noise, holding Edlyn close. Vanora came in, gripping a candle in her hand.

"To the cellar! Quickly!" she instructed in hushed tones, motioning for them to follow.

With Edlyn braced against him, Maddock rushed after the old woman. They hurried through the main room of the home while more forceful beating on the front door rang in their ears.

"Open immediately, or we shall break the door down!" a different voice declared.

Edlyn nearly cried out with alarm. It was the voice of Sheriff Hurst.

"I know, Edlyn. The sheriff is here," Maddock whispered, reading her thoughts.

Vanora led them to the back of the house, where she stopped, reached out to a tall cabinet that stood against the wall, and pulled upon it. Unexpectedly, the cabinet swung toward her like a door on hinges, revealing the entrance to an unlit passageway behind.

"There are eleven steps down," Vanora told Maddock. "Hurry!"

Maddock carried Edlyn into the secret passageway and began cautiously descending the stairs. The cabinet was quickly closed behind them, leaving the cellar in blackness. They heard Vanora scurry away.

"There are five soldiers outside: three in front, including the sheriff, and two guarding the back," Maddock said in Edlyn's ear, taking another careful step down. He paused and seemed to be searching around with his feet, confirming that they were at the base of the stairs.

"I...I can stand," Edlyn told him.

"Are you sure?"

"I am sure."

Maddock set Edlyn down but kept one arm around her. Clinging to each other in the cold and dark, they listened. From above, they heard the muffled thudding finally cease. The front door had been opened. Someone began talking.

"I should have known," Maddock muttered, his breathing strong and steady.

"Kn...known?" Edlyn repeated.

"That Peyton would betray us," Maddock said bitterly. "He has been gone for the past two days, and now it is clear why. He went and turned us in to the king."

"Surely...you are wrong. He w...would not do that."

"Edlyn, the storm has grown worse. No one would venture into these dangerous, remote hills without good reason. Having Sheriff Hurst show up here tonight cannot be coincidence."

"But that does not...mean it was Peyton who—"

"Who else would it have been?" Maddock interrupted. "Peyton was angry—angry and worried that I might have put them at risk. After being turned in once for reward money, I should have known that it would happen again."

Edlyn stayed silent, not wanting to believe him. But as she heard soldiers stomping across the floor above, her heart sank. She knew Maddock was right. There was no other explanation for why the king's soldiers would have hunted down Vanora's home.

"All of the soldiers are inside now," Maddock told her, listening to the floor boards creak. "And the sheriff is coming this way."

Maddock pulled Edlyn back from the staircase and put one hand upon his dagger. When the sheriff's steps drew near to the cabinet that guarded the cellar's entrance, Edlyn instinctively slid even closer to Maddock.

"You are freezing," Maddock noted with worry.

"I am...fine. I am just not quite...as strong as..."

She did not finish her sentence, for the front door of the house opened again. Another person—a person with familiar, strong footsteps—walked inside.

"Peyton!" Vanora exclaimed with relief. "I have been concerned about you! Why did you stay out in the storm? Where have you been?"

"It took longer than expected to find the herbs I was searching for," Peyton replied.

Peyton took a few more steps before coming to a halt.

"Ah, Peyton, there you are," Sheriff Hurst's voice carried through the home. "Good evening."

"Good evening, Sheriff Hurst."

Edlyn shook her head sorrowfully. The sheriff and Peyton knew each other by name. There was no longer any doubt that it was Peyton who had betrayed them.

"Peyton, have you met my new deputy?" the sheriff went on pleasantly. "I do not believe that you two had a chance to chat when you were at the castle last."

"Good evening," said another man, who sounded younger than the sheriff. "My name is Briac."

"Good evening, Briac," Peyton flatly replied.

Peyton could be heard advancing farther into the house.

"Well, it is good to see that you are alright, Peyton," the sheriff said. "We have been expecting your arrival for several days now."

"The storm has delayed my journey," Peyton stated unapologetically.

"Yes. It must not be easy to navigate these hills in this weather," the sheriff politely carried on. "Even for one as skilled as you."

There was a noise, as if Peyton had pulled a chair from the table and sat down by the fire. "No, it is not easy, Sheriff, especially not with my wagon. And it would be foolish to try."

"Of course. The king and queen will understand. They have simply been curious to know what has kept you."

Peyton spoke carefully, "Was there some other reason for my delay suspected?"

The sheriff laughed. "No, no. They are just anxious for your regular arrival."

"I see. Well, as I said, I am only waiting for the storm to clear so I can make it down these hills safely with my wagon."

"A wise decision," the sheriff proclaimed. "Do you wish that I convey this message to the king and queen?"

"Yes, Sheriff. Tell them that I shall make my delivery as soon as I can."

"Excellent. We shall be off to relay your message immediately," Sheriff Hurst replied. "Come, Briac. Come, everyone."

There was movement of the men heading toward the front door.

"It is quite a storm out there, Sheriff Hurst," Vanora noted. "I am amazed that you were able to reach us tonight."

Sheriff Hurst chuckled. "We have our ways."

The front door was opened.

"Oh, there is one other thing," the sheriff added. "You have not, by chance, seen any strangers— peasants—in these hills in recent days, have you?"

"Peasants?" Peyton repeated.

"A young man and woman," Sheriff Hurst explained casually.

There was a tense pause. Edlyn caught her breath. Beside her, Maddock had become very still.

Peyton finally spoke again, "You expect such a duo to be wandering these hills during a storm like this?"

"No, of course not," Sheriff Hurst hastily answered. "But if you see anyone unusual, I would like to be informed immediately."

"Of course," Vanora promised him. "We will keep an eye out."

There was more movement. The footsteps faded. The front door was closed.

Edlyn dared to breathe. "Maddock, what—"

She stopped short when she felt Maddock's finger being pressed lightly upon her lips.

"They have not left yet," he whispered. "I am sure that they are still outside, watching this house."

The two of them again fell into an uneasy silence. Minutes passed. From above, there came the sound of Vanora approaching the back of the home.

"Do not open the cellar entrance," Maddock muttered, as if willing Vanora to sense what he was saying. "Do not give this hiding place away."

"Mother," Peyton suddenly said with deliberateness, "come see this leak near the front window. We will need to repair it tonight before it worsens."

Vanora stopped and walked the other way. Edlyn felt Maddock's body relax.

"You see, Maddock? P...Peyton did not turn us in," Edlyn told him.

"Perhaps, but Peyton clearly must work for the king and queen. Do not forget Ailith's warning about being too trusting." Maddock listened again, and then he reached down and lifted her in his arms. "Come. I can hear the sheriff and his soldiers departing. The home is safe now."

As Maddock began climbing the stairs, the cabinet was thrown back, flooding the cellar with light.

"Hurry, Maddock. We must get Edlyn warm," Vanora called down. "The cellar is far too cold for her to have been in there for so long."

Maddock carried Edlyn past Vanora and into the main part of the house. On the other side of the room, Peyton was seated near the fireplace, leaning forward and studying the flames. When Maddock entered with Edlyn, Peyton got up and motioned to his chair.

"Let her sit here."

Maddock carried Edlyn across the room and helped her into Peyton's chair, which he slid closer to the fireplace. Edlyn shivered and hunched forward, closing her eyes while her body began absorbing the warmth. She felt someone place a blanket over her shoulders, and she looked up. It was Peyton. He gave her a brief look before walking to the opposite corner of the room.

"Well, that was a most unwelcome visit," Vanora proclaimed, shutting the cabinet to conceal the cellar's entrance. With a perturbed shake of her head, she stepped toward her son and spoke quietly, "Surely the king and queen understand that the storm would delay your trip."

"I have no doubt that they do," Peyton replied, not bothering to lower his voice. "I think we all know that inquiring after me cannot be the real reason Sheriff Hurst came here tonight." Peyton cast a hard look at Maddock. "Perhaps Maddock can explain why the king and queen care so much about finding two peasants that they would send the sheriff and their highest-ranking soldiers out into a violent storm to search for them."

"Peyton," Vanora began uncomfortably, glancing at the others, "they have done nothing wrong to—"

"I, for one, would find Maddock's explanation very interesting," Peyton went on, just as severely. "For as we all know, there will surely be a harsh punishment brought down upon any who are found aiding the wanted duo, even if those who gave the help did not realize that they were assisting outlaws."

"I suppose we all have things that we want explained." Maddock let his angry eyes meet Peyton's. "Perhaps, Peyton, you should explain why you work for those as evil as the king and queen."

"Maddock, stop it," Edlyn snapped.

Peyton's glare was unrelenting. "Working for the king and queen is my job, Maddock. At least I do not put the lives of others in danger by my actions." He gestured toward Edlyn. "Can you say the same?"

"Working for the king and queen does endanger the lives of others," Maddock fumed. "The people in Nereth are—"

"Stop it!" Edlyn pushed herself to her feet, fed up. "Stop this, both of you! There..."

But Edlyn could not finish. Weak and exhausted, her head became light and her vision faded. As she made a blind reach for the chair to support herself, she heard footsteps. Someone grabbed her by the waist, and another person supported her arms. She was assisted down onto the chair. Gradually, her vision returned, and then Edlyn saw both Maddock and Peyton before her.

"Let go of me," Edlyn told them.

With a look of surprise, Peyton released his hold on Edlyn's arms. Maddock slowly let go of her waist.

Edlyn kept her voice strong as she spoke to the young men, "You two foolishly fight over nothing. No one here has done anything wrong." She turned to Vanora. "Yes, Maddock is wanted by Sheriff Hurst—by the king and queen—but he is hunted unjustly. They are after Maddock because..." Edlyn broke off, catching herself before she possibly said too much. She quickly started again, "Maddock is wanted for striving to rescue a friend from unjust imprisonment and for saving me from a fate worse than death." Catching her breath, Edlyn looked right at Peyton. "Maddock has not put me in danger. It is by my own choice that I am with him."

Worn out, Edlyn finished by leaning forward and staring miserably at the flames. Continuing to observe her, Peyton returned to the far corner of the room. Maddock then walked back to the fireplace.

"Edlyn was gravely sick," Maddock said after a while. "I had no choice but to seek out your help to save her life. I would not have put you in danger otherwise."

There was more silence before Peyton cleared his throat and explained:

"It is true that I work for the king and queen. I harvest herbs and other plants that are only found in these hills, and I deliver them to the castle. But that is all I do for them, and I only do the work so that my mother and I can survive."

Growing strengthened by the warmth of the fire, Edlyn focused again on Peyton and Vanora. "Though you work for the king and queen, you did not turn us in to Sheriff Hurst. And you did not even know what it was we were hunted for. Thank you."

"I may work for the king and queen, but it does not mean that I support them. Any enemy of theirs is likely a friend of mine," Peyton replied.

Maddock looked at Peyton. Peyton casually leaned against the wall and gave Maddock a slight nod. Maddock understandingly tipped his head in return.

"Well, now you know a little of our story," Vanora said with a sad smile. She faced Maddock. "And now we know a little of yours, young man. You dare to attempt to rescue a friend who is imprisoned by the king and queen?"

Maddock's eyes glistened in the firelight. "I shall not rest until I have freed Ronan or died trying."

His tone made Edlyn shudder.

"That is a brave task you undertake," Vanora went on. "And a dangerous one."

Maddock spoke resolutely, "That is why I intend to finish it alone."

"No," Edlyn protested. "I am coming with you, Maddock. You cannot—"

Vanora raised her hands. "Quiet, everyone. Quiet. These issues understandably trigger emotional responses in us all, but squabbling tonight will not help. We must band together, for it is true that we have all been victims of the king and queen's rule in some way." Vanora's eyes became distant. "Yes, these eastern hills were once a prosperous farming community, but even this land could not remain safe from oppression forever. Once rumors reached the castle about the unique plants that grow upon these hills—and the medicines and potions that can be created from them—the king and queen began demanding portions of the farmers' harvests. It has continued this way for centuries. Those who refuse to cooperate are imprisoned. Of those who stay, many die of starvation." She broke off mournfully and motioned to her son. "It is only because our knowledge about this area's vegetation is deemed so valuable that we are allowed to keep our farm."

"The king and queen have no choice but to let us stay," Peyton clarified with a slight tone of satisfaction. "My mother and I are the only ones left in Nereth who understand the secrets of what grows upon these ancient hills. It is a knowledge that has been passed down through my mother's family for generations."

Maddock stroked his chin. "What do the king and queen do with the plants that you bring to them?"

"We do not know," Vanora admitted remorsefully. "I often wonder if we are doing the right thing, obeying their orders as we do."

"You do not have a choice," Edlyn pointed out gently, growing stronger from the fire. "You are only doing it to survive. You have to comply with the king and queen's wishes."

"Comply? Hardly. But at least that is what the king and queen believe we do," Peyton remarked.

Maddock tipped his head with interest. "So you do not share all of your knowledge with the king and queen?"

Peyton shrugged. "I have never even met them. I only bring the deliveries to the castle. The less the king and queen know about the plants—and the less they realize how much they do not know—the better. I do not go out of my way to explain more."

"It is the only thing we can do to try and prevent the king and queen from using our ancient knowledge for evil purposes," Vanora added. "We do not know for what reason the king and queen so regularly demand what grows upon these hills, but we do our best to keep any potentially dangerous vegetation—or knowledge—from getting into their hands."

"That is a brave thing you do, secretly defying the king and queen like that," Edlyn told them with admiration.

Peyton eyed her. "Others have done things far more brave than I."

Edlyn paused, colored, and looked away.

"But one day, we will not have to fear," Vanora declared. "One day, the descendent of Tiernan will return. All will be made right in Nereth."

Edlyn peeked at Maddock before realizing what she was doing. Maddock noticed her and turned away, but not before the silent exchange was observed by Peyton.

"My mother's statement about Tiernan's descendent catches your attention, I see," Peyton remarked, looking at her.

Edlyn shifted. "It catches everyone's interest, does it not? Maddock and I discussed the ancient legend once. That is all."

"No doubt you and Maddock discussed many things on your journey." Peyton commented. "Tell me, Edlyn, what was this fate worse than death that you say Maddock saved you from?"

Edlyn faltered uncomfortably. "It is nothing now."

"Sheriff Hurst wanted Edlyn," Maddock answered for her, his dark eyes narrowed and focused on the fire.

Peyton's expression changed. "I...I am sorry, Edlyn. I did not mean to say anything to cause you distress."

Edlyn sat back. "Your words do not distress me, Peyton, only the sheriff does. Sheriff Hurst treated me like a possession or a prized steed. There may be some women who would be honored by such attentions, but I am not one of them."

Peyton kept watching her, saying nothing.

"Goodness me, Edlyn!" Vanora suddenly exclaimed. "What have I been doing, letting you stay up for so long? You must get to bed!"

Edlyn did not want the conversation to end, yet she could not ignore how fatigued she had become. She stood up from the table. "Goodnight, everyone."

With the light of the fire to guide her, Edlyn began walking toward her bedroom. She listed only once, but it was enough that Peyton reached out to brace her. Edlyn gave him a thankful nod, glanced at Maddock, and then, with a sigh, stepped into her room and shut the door.

10

"What are you doing up so late, young man?" Vanora whispered.

"I could not sleep. I needed to see how she was doing," Maddock replied.

Edlyn shifted and opened her eyes. Her bedroom was dark except for a faint glow of embers in the fireplace. She could barely make out the movements of those who stood near the door.

"She is doing better, Maddock," Vanora was saying. "Much better."

"So she is out of danger?"

"Yes, Maddock, I believe that she is out of danger. Of course, she still needs more time to fully regain her strength," Vanora added, "but the worst is over."

"Vanora," Maddock's voice caught slightly, "I do not know what I would have done...what would have happened had you not...thank you."

"Edlyn has a strong and determined spirit, and she has something to live for. Those are the things that healed her, Maddock, not me," she told him. "Now you should get some rest. You have barely slept since you arrived here."

"Yes. I will leave."

But instead of retreating, Maddock came toward the bed. In the darkness, Edlyn felt him reach down and put his hand upon hers.

"Sleep well, Edlyn," he said softly.

His firm hand let go. Edlyn heard him step from the room. Vanora stoked the fire, and then the old woman slipped out and closed the door behind her. All was still. Edlyn rolled onto her side. Through the window, she saw the very first hints of morning light appearing. The storm was clearing. With a contented sigh, she closed her eyes and drifted off into a peaceful sleep.

***

The sound of a wagon rolling past caused Edlyn to yawn and awaken. Outside the window, the sun shone brightly in a clear sky. With the warmth of the sunlight soaking into her skin, Edlyn sat up and stretched. Her mind felt sharp and clear as she took a deep, refreshing breath and then gazed out the window. She spotted Peyton near the barn, loading supplies into the back of a wagon. From where the sun sat in the sky above him, Edlyn realized that it was already early afternoon.

The clanking of pots from the main part of the house was another reminder that the others had long been awake. Edlyn got up from bed and changed into the freshly washed gown that hung next to the fireplace. After securing her necklace and pulling her hair into a braid, Edlyn opened the bedroom door and stepped out.

Vanora, who was cooking something in a cauldron over the fire, looked up and smiled. "Well, good afternoon, my dear. This is quite a welcome surprise. You must be feeling better?"

Edlyn nodded. "I am."

"It shows, for your color is back, and your eyes have some life to them," Vanora remarked with satisfaction. "A very good sight, indeed."

"It is nice to be almost myself again," Edlyn agreed.

Vanora scooped soup from the cauldron and poured it into a bowl. "You woke just in time for dinner. I insist that you eat a proper meal. Sit down."

"Thank you," Edlyn said, taking a place at the table, her stomach growling.

Vanora placed the bowl in front of her. "Here you are. I want you to have all of that."

As Edlyn settled in to eat, the front door opened. Peyton stepped inside, stopping in his tracks when he saw Edlyn.

"You are awake," he remarked bluntly.

Edlyn replied, "I am awake."

"And looking well, too," Vanora added while setting a platter of bread and cheese next to her. "Do you not agree, Peyton?"

Peyton remained in the doorway. "Yes. I agree."

Edlyn felt her checks get warm, and she made herself busy eating.

"Come, Peyton, you also need dinner," Vanora instructed her son, motioning to the table. "You have a long trip before you."

Edlyn raised her head. "You are leaving, Peyton?"

He came to the table and sat across from her. "The storm has cleared. I can delay no longer. It is time for me to make my journey to the castle."

"How long will you be gone?"

Peyton swallowed a bite of bread before peering at her. "Not long, I hope."

Vanora returned to the table and set another bowl of soup in front of an empty chair. "I hate to wake Maddock. He must be exhausted. The poor boy has not made a sound in hours." She looked toward the small staircase at the opposite side of the room. "But he needs dinner, for he has hardly eaten a thing in days. I am sure his appetite will improve once he sees how well you are doing, Edlyn." Vanora moved to the base of the stairs and called quietly up to the second story. "Maddock? Dinner is ready."

"He is not there," Peyton announced.

Both Vanora and Edlyn turned to him.

"I was upstairs earlier to get my supplies," Peyton explained. "The bed has not been slept in."

Vanora sighed and looked out the window. "He must have slept in the barn. I told him that was not necessary but—"

Peyton interrupted, "He is not in the barn, either."

Edlyn slowly set her food down. With a lump forming in her throat, she stared across the table at Peyton. "Maddock is not here anymore, is he?" she asked, barely above a whisper.

"I do not believe that he is."

Edlyn looked over at Vanora, who turned from the window with the same shocked expression as Edlyn knew was on her own face. As the terrible realization crashed down upon her, Edlyn stood, ran to the front door, and threw it open.

"He left," she said aloud to no one. "He left without me."

Edlyn stumbled out into the sunlight. Tears spilled freely down her face as she spun around, gazing dazedly at the barren, empty hills that surrounded her.

Maddock was gone. She was alone.

Edlyn ran farther from the house, grappling to comprehend what happened. Maddock had abandoned her. He was headed alone toward dangers that no one understood—dangers he could not survive—and she had never even told him goodbye. Overcome, Edlyn began to sob as she dropped to her knees.

"Edlyn, it was for the best."

Edlyn raised her eyes. Peyton was coming toward her.

"Maddock knew that I wanted to go with him. He knew, yet he left me here," Edlyn declared through her tears. "How could he do such a heartless, stupid, dangerous thing?"

Peyton knelt across from her. "I am sure that he did what he thought was best for you."

"But what about what was best for him? He will die, Peyton! Maddock will die if he attempts to carry out his mission alone!"

"As I said, I do not believe that Maddock was thinking of himself when he made his decision."

Edlyn moaned and dropped her head, too overwhelmed to respond.

"Edlyn, you are still weak. You need to go back inside," Peyton remarked after a few moments. Without waiting for her to reply, he put a wide hand around Edlyn's arm and practically lifted her to her feet. "Take care of yourself while I am gone. Take care of yourself, if for no other reason than that was what Maddock wanted."

His words cut Edlyn to the core. She wrung her shaking hands and wept in silence.

"Edlyn, my dear, please come in."

Wiping the tears from her face, Edlyn saw Vanora watching worriedly from the doorway. The old woman next spoke to her son:

"You should finish your meal, too."

Peyton released Edlyn and gestured to the sky. "I cannot. It is already late. I must prepare the horses and be off."

With a last glance at Edlyn, Peyton turned and headed for the stable. Edlyn watched after him, her mind racing.

"Edlyn, come rest," Vanora urged again.

Edlyn's eyes continued following Peyton. "I just need a few moments to myself."

Giving Vanora a forced smile, Edlyn began walking toward a grove of trees not far away.

***

Peyton snapped the reins, urging on the team of horses that drew his wagon down the hillside. The evening was waning, and it would not be long before he would have to stop to set up camp for the night.

Just before reaching another bend, the wagon jolted when its back wheels rolled over loose rocks. The horses whinnied and reared up, jarring the wagon again. There was a cracking sound as one of the back wheels snapped, dropping the corner of the wagon into the dirt. The wagon came to an abrupt stop.

With an exasperated grunt, Peyton set the reins onto the seat beside him and leapt down to the earth. He walked to the back of the wagon, reached for the thick cloth that covered his load, and flipped it back. He nearly yelled in surprise when he found Edlyn hiding among his tools. She hastily sat up and brushed her hair from her face.

"Hello, Peyton."

His mouth fell open slightly.

"I am sorry about this," Edlyn went on sheepishly. "I did not know what else—"

"Edlyn, what are you doing here?" Peyton demanded.

Edlyn tipped her head. "I am trying to find Maddock before he attempts to invade the castle, of course."

With a sigh, Peyton reached out and assisted her to the ground. "Edlyn, Maddock left you for a reason. He did not want you with him."

"I do not care what he wanted," Edlyn retorted, trying to ignore the hurt caused by Peyton's words. "Maddock needs someone with him, whether he wants the help or not."

"And you think that you can provide the assistance he needs?" Peyton eyed her. "You think that you will be able to help him invade the castle, get past the king's soldiers, break someone out of the dungeon, and escape to safety?"

Edlyn put her hands on her hips. "I may not be the fiercest warrior in the kingdom, Peyton, but at least I am trying."

Peyton motioned up the mountain. "Does my mother know that you are gone?"

Edlyn cringed. "No."

"A fine way to treat her, after all she has done for you."

"Peyton, please believe me when I say that I am extremely sorry. I know how it feels to have someone abandon you," she insisted, her voice quivering. "But I had no choice. Maddock's life is in danger."

Peyton's stern expression relented slightly. "I need to take you back. My mother will be frantic with worry. You are supposed to be resting and getting better, not out roaming the mountains at night."

"Take me back? You do not have time for that, and even if you did have the time, I would not let you. You men seem to forget that I have my own will and opinions, and I will not simply do as you tell me to."

Peyton raised an eyebrow.

"Besides," Edlyn went on, her cheeks growing warm under his gaze, "your mother will surely realize what I have done. I can only hope that she will forgive me one day."

Peyton crossed his arms. "You may have your own will, Edlyn, but so do I, and I am not going to enable you to do something foolish."

"Fine. I shall carry on by myself."

Edlyn spun on her heels and began marching down the path.

"Edlyn, do not be ridiculous."

She did not bother turning back. "I am not being ridiculous. I am trying to help Maddock, and I am losing time arguing with you."

She heard the sound of Peyton jogging up behind her. He grabbed her by the arm. "It is growing dark. Regardless of what you may want to do, you cannot continue safely tonight."

Edlyn stopped and peered uncertainly around them. The shadows were growing long, and the sounds of unseen creatures were beginning to carry through the evening air. She shivered in the cool breeze.

"We can set up camp here. I will fix the wagon before it gets dark," Peyton went on.

"And tomorrow?" Edlyn pressed.

"We will decide when the morning comes."

Edlyn gave only a slight nod in consent.

"That will not do, Edlyn. I can guess what might be going through your mind. You must promise me that you will not try to sneak off during the night."

"I cannot do that," Edlyn admitted. "With every minute we rest here, Maddock is getting farther ahead."

"You really would try to continue on your own tonight?"

"Yes."

"Edlyn, you will be no help to Maddock if you are dead," Peyton tried again. "These hills contain dangers that you do not understand. I have lived my entire life here, and I promise that you will not be able to navigate these hills on your own—especially not at night."

"What else can I do, Peyton? Maddock would do the same for me."

Peyton dropped his head and breathed out resignedly. He then motioned behind him. "We must work fast to fix the wagon before nightfall. Then we will set out together."

***

"Here. Take this."

Peyton reached across the wagon seat, handed Edlyn his coat, and then faced forward again and lightly snapped the reins over the horses' backs.

"But what about you?" Edlyn inquired, fingering the coat's fur-lined leather.

"You need the coat more than I do," he replied in a way that made it clear it would be pointless to argue.

Edlyn gratefully draped the large coat over her shoulders. She sat back, staying quiet while the wagon methodically continued down the rocky path, the silvery light of the full moon lighting the way.

"You are uneasy," Peyton remarked after a few minutes.

"I worry for Maddock. Who knows where he might be by now? He got a significant head start on us."

"And he can travel faster on foot over this terrain than we can by wagon, you also want to say," Peyton guessed.

"Yes, but I would not be traveling safely at all, were it not for you. Thank you for what you are doing for me."

"You made it rather impossible to do otherwise."

Edlyn laughed, the sound echoing off the mountainside. The faintest hint of a smile appeared on Peyton's face. More time passed before Edlyn saw him turn toward her again.

"Where did you come from, Edlyn? Prior to becoming wanted throughout the kingdom, I mean."

"Nowhere of interest. I have been a serf since I was young."

"Your parents?"

"My mother died in childbirth. My father was killed when I was eleven," she answered quickly. "What happened to your father? How did he die?"

"The doctor never determined what made him fall so rapidly ill." Peyton was looking straight ahead. "He was well one day and dead two evenings later. I was eighteen."

Edlyn shivered and pulled the coat more tightly around her. "I am sorry, Peyton."

They fell into silence.

"So it is true that Sheriff Hurst really wanted to make you his bride?" Peyton eventually inquired.

"Sheriff Hurst is a horrible, selfish man."

"He is rich, and he has good connections."

"Are you suggesting that nothing else should matter?" Edlyn challenged. "Why should money and importance be all that a woman aspires to in a marriage? Can a woman not want love and happiness? Or respect?"

Peyton shot her a sideways glance. "You think that pining after a wanderer who is on a secret journey—and nearly being brought upon your deathbed because of him—is happiness?"

Edlyn turned away. "I am pining after no one."

"As you say. But I have seen the way that the young man from the Colleland watches you."

Edlyn did a double take. "How did you know that Maddock is from the Colleland?"

"His accent is unmistakable to those who recognize it."

"How...how do you..."

"My father was from the Colleland."

"What?" Edlyn whispered.

Peyton pulled on the reins, bringing the wagon to a stop. "Years ago, my father came to Nereth from the Colleland. It was a last, desperate attempt to locate his adopted brother, who had gone missing. My father's search was futile, but he chose to remain in Nereth because he met and fell in love with my mother. After I was born, my parents took over the farm from my mother's family. I grew up hearing my father's stories about the Colleland."

Edlyn's heart was racing. Peyton's story confirmed what she had always believed: that at least one more from the Colleland had found Nereth. And if there had been one, Edlyn was certain that there were others—even if the Langerlen had never known of them.

"Peyton," Edlyn began, swallowing hard, "did your father know of more?"

"More?"

"More from the Colleland who found Nereth. Did your father know of them?"

Peyton leaned toward her. "You are breathing hard, and you are pale. Are you alright?"

"Peyton, please, I need you to answer me. Did your father ever speak about others from the Colleland who found Nereth? Did he know where they dwelt or who they were?"

"No, Edlyn, my father never spoke of others," Peyton watched her peculiarly. "If he knew of more people from the Colleland ever being in this kingdom, he did not say so."

Edlyn's disappointment was like being struck in the gut. She dropped her head, fighting to suppress frustrated tears.

"Edlyn, what is wrong? Can I do something to help—"

"You can do nothing."

There was a tense break in the conversation.

"Edlyn, this day has been long enough," Peyton finally declared. "We should stop for the night."

"No. You promised that we would—"

"You and I both know that we are not going to catch Maddock at this rate. And I am not going to let you become sick again in a futile attempt to do so."

Before Edlyn could reply, there came a noise from the shadows nearby. Peyton leapt to his feet and skillfully threw his axe into the darkness. Edlyn heard the sickening sound of the weapon striking human flesh. Without a word, Peyton hurriedly got down from the wagon and ran off in the direction from which the noise had come, disappearing into the night.

"Peyton?" Edlyn whispered. Trembling from shock, she got out of the wagon and called again, "Peyton?"

Everything remained unnervingly quiet. Edlyn was about to follow after Peyton when he reappeared into the moonlight. His axe, tinged with blood, was hanging again by his side. He was dragging the body of a man who wore the uniform of a king's soldier.

"It appears that the king's soldiers search these hills for you and Maddock still. He was about to strike," Peyton said grimly, tossing the body into a deep crack between two towering boulders. "We must hide the corpse and move from this place."

"You attacked...without...knowing what moved in the darkness," Edlyn stammered.

"It was a human step, and only an enemy would be stalking us at night."

"But you did not know for sure," Edlyn went on, watching as Peyton started covering the body with branches. "What if this man had been Maddock?"

Peyton put his eyes on hers. "Then I would not have heard him."

Peyton resumed his grisly task. Only once the body was concealed did he speak again:

"We must hurry, Edlyn." Peyton took her hand and pulled her back to the wagon. "We will let the animals finish disposing of the evidence."

Still reeling, Edlyn allowed Peyton to lift her back into the wagon. When he was about to climb up beside her, they both started hearing several men talking in the distance.

"It is as I feared," Peyton uttered in a low voice. "That soldier was not alone. There are more of them headed this way."

"I will hide," Edlyn told him, jumping out of the wagon.

"No." Peyton reached out, preventing her from bolting off. "Even if they search my wagon and let me pass, I will surely be watched for the rest of my journey. With the king's soldiers trailing me, I could not reunite with you. You would be left on your own, and if you did not succumb to the elements or the animals first, you would be hunted down and captured."

"But what else can we do? If they find me with you, you will be arrested!"

Peyton looked around, and then he focused intensely again on her. "Edlyn, I have grown up learning the secrets of what grows in these hills. I understand their powers better than anyone in the kingdom, even my mother. So I ask: do you trust me?"

"What?"

"Edlyn, do you trust me?" he repeated urgently, placing his large hands on her shoulders. "Will you trust what I am about to ask you to do?"

The talking of the approaching soldiers was getting louder. Edlyn peeked apprehensively off into the distance before she nodded.

"Yes, Peyton. I trust you."

Without another word, Peyton ran to a tree and started scraping a small amount of its bark into his palm. "Edlyn, do you see that weed growing near the rocks behind you?" he called out quietly while he worked. "Grab as much of it as you can, and bring it here."

Edlyn sprinted to the rocks, crouched down, and hastily began digging up a green plant with her fingers.

"No, not those," Peyton said, watching what she was doing. "The smaller plant. The one with the wide leaves."

Edlyn bent forward and stared more closely at the vegetation beneath her feet. Only then did she notice the subtle difference between the plants that were growing there. She pulled up as many of the needed leaves as she could find and then rushed to Peyton's side.

Peyton had started funneling the crushed tree bark into his leather water flask. "How much did you get?"

Edlyn held out her hand for him to see.

His brow furrowed. "We shall have to hope that it will last long enough."

Peyton took the leaves from her hand, ground them between his strong fingers, and slipped them inside the flask. He next reached into the pocket of his vest and pulled out a small vial of white powder, which he poured into the drink. Edlyn watched as he closed the flask and shook it vigorously.

"Edlyn, you need to drink this," he told her, holding out the flask. "All of this."

"Drink it?" she repeated warily.

The commotion of men talking, accompanied by horses whinnying and dogs barking, was getting louder. The search party was nearly upon them.

"Yes, Edlyn. Drink this now."

"What will it—"

"Edlyn, drink it."

Peyton pushed the flask into her hands. Edlyn raised it to her lips. After a last look at him, she put her head back and swallowed. The taste was so bitter that it nearly caused her to vomit. Once she was done, she coughed and handed the flask back to him.

"Peyton, what is..."

She did not finish. Her feet had gone cold, causing her to catch her breath in terrified surprise. As the chill hauntingly began ascending her body, she looked at Peyton, eyes wide with fear.

Peyton reached out to hold her. "You will be alright, Edlyn."

Her legs gave out, and she dropped weakly into Peyton's arms. Edlyn stared up at him as the freezing sensation moved into her torso and past her heart. She let out an involuntary cough. The cold kept traveling steadily through her neck and finally into her head. For an instant, there was a feeling of falling. Then there was nothing.

11

"Dead?"

"Yes," Peyton repeated. "Dead."

Edlyn foggily began to hear a conversation, which was taking place close by. As her senses cleared, she realized that she was lying flat on her back with her eyes shut. Her body was cold. Edlyn attempted to sit up but, to her alarm, found that she could not move. She was completely paralyzed.

There was a rustling noise immediately above her as something lying on top of her body was pulled away.

"Who did you say she was?" the man speaking with Peyton demanded.

Peyton's recognizable footsteps approached. "She was my mother's second cousin."

"She died young," the man remarked.

"Yes, Briac, she did," Peyton replied.

Peyton said the man's name with emphasis, catching Edlyn's attention. She realized that Peyton was speaking to Sheriff Hurst's new deputy—the same man who had accompanied the sheriff to Vanora and Peyton's house during the recent storm.

"She was a beautiful girl. You must be sad to no longer have her company, eh?" someone else remarked.

Several other men laughed appreciatively in response. Edlyn was struck with a rush of fear, wondering how many soldiers were surrounding the wagon.

"What did she die of?" Briac inquired as the others' laughter faded.

"A stomach infection."

Briac's breathing grew louder, and the smells of campfire and leather filled Edlyn's nose. He was leaning right over her. Edlyn attempted to hold her breath only to find that she had no control over her own respirations, which were so slow as to be nearly imperceptible.

"Well, if you and your mother could not heal her, I am sure no one else would have been able to do so," Briac commented, hovering only inches from Edlyn's face.

"She was already sick when she came to us a month ago," Peyton explained. "It was her family's hope that we could nurse her back to health. It was, unfortunately, too late."

Edlyn felt Briac's hand press her neck for several seconds. Next, he lifted her arm by the wrist and then let it drop. As her arm slammed down by her side, Edlyn had the involuntary impulse to cry out with pain. However, her body remained still and silent.

"She is newly dead," Briac observed.

"She passed only a few hours ago," Peyton sounded unaffected.

There was more rustling as the cover was placed over Edlyn once more. Briac and the soldiers had been fooled.

"You choose a rather strange hour to be out delivering bodies, Peyton," Briac noted.

"I wanted to bring the girl to her family as soon as possible, and I was already planning to make my delivery to the castle."

Briac let out a wry laugh. "I suppose that I cannot judge you for being out late. The sheriff has kept us out here, combing the hills for those two wanted peasants."

"It seems an odd thing for the king's soldiers to be spending their time doing," Peyton commented.

"I have never heard of anything like it before."

"The two you seek must be wanted for something very serious or very unusual," Peyton continued.

"I do not know the reason they are hunted, but it is what Sheriff Hurst has ordered in the name of the king and queen, and so I obey," Briac replied with a sigh. "I shall not delay your journey any longer, Peyton. I am sure the king and queen are anxiously awaiting your delivery."

"I am sure that they are."

"Meanwhile, we must be off," Briac said. "For in addition to hunting two peasants, we also must locate a member of our own party, who has apparently gone missing."

Edlyn cringed at Briac's words, and her body actually moved in response. Very cautiously, she tried moving again. She was able to wiggle her toes and fingers.

"Come, men!" Briac shouted, walking away from the wagon. "It is time to depart!"

Conversations, dogs barking, and the snorts of horses were heard. Over the commotion, Edlyn detected Peyton's footsteps coming closer. She felt his hand rest over her arm, monitoring the pulse in her wrist.

"Edlyn, the potion is wearing off," he whispered.

Edlyn moved her fingers, letting him know that she had heard and understood. Peyton quickly removed his hand and walked away. Edlyn felt the wagon tip to one side as he climbed into the front seat. With a snap of the reins, Peyton made a sound to his horses. The wagon lurched and began slowly rolling downhill. Meanwhile, Edlyn kept flexing her hands and feet, encouraging the sensation to return. She attempted some deep breaths, and the restrictive coldness that pressed upon her chest gradually dissipated, allowing her to control her own respirations once more.

Suddenly, farther up the path, the soldiers' dogs started barking excitedly. Then men began to shout:

"He is dead!"

"Someone murdered him!"

Peyton made a sharp yell to his horses, and the team broke into a gallop. The wagon picked up speed, bumping harshly over the uneven ground and tossing Edlyn about in the back. Above the wagon noise, Edlyn began hearing the ominous sound of more horses— Briac and his soldiers were coming after Peyton.

"Peyton, halt in the name of the king!" Briac ordered, riding closer. "Stop, or I shall tell my men to attack!"

The pursuing soldiers raced closer. There was more barking from the dogs. Men shouted. Horses whinnied. Swords were unsheathed. Noise completely surrounded the wagon as the chase continued.

"Peyton, if you value your life—and the life of your mother—you will stop!" Briac called out fiercely.

Peyton let out an angry growl and brought the wagon to a halt. Edlyn barely managed to suppress a grunt as the abrupt motion jostled her around before she became still.

"Peyton, raise your arms and step down slowly," Briac commanded, breathing hard.

The wagon tilted. Peyton's boots landed on the ground.

"Is there a problem?" Peyton calmly inquired.

"A problem?" Briac repeated incredulously, dismounting his horse. "Our dogs discovered the missing solider lying dead only a few feet from where you were just now. The corpse has a skillfully placed axe wound in his chest. So it is I who asks you, Peyton, is there a problem?"

Edlyn fought to open her eyes. Her vision was spotty, but through the cover that was upon her, she could make out traces of movement caused by those who were near the wagon.

"I am sorry about your solider, sir," Peyton told Briac. "It is an unfortunate discovery, indeed. But an axe is an extremely common tool in these parts. Everyone carries one. I am afraid it will not help you identify who might have killed him."

No longer slowed by the potion, Edlyn's heart began pounding. She waited tensely. Her body hurt from the position she was forced to stay in, and it was taking all her effort to keep her breathing shallow and quiet.

"Then explain why you tried to flee," she heard Briac demand.

"Flee?" Peyton repeated. "Your dogs' barking startled my team of horses. They bolted. It was all I could do to keep control of the wagon and prevent it from careening down the steep hillside."

As the sensation continued to return to Edlyn's aching body, she realized that there was something against her torso. She glanced down. It was Peyton's axe.

Peyton spoke again, "I assume that I may put my arms down?"

"Do nothing foolish," Briac warned.

"I have no reason to do so, sir."

Briac walked forward. "Peyton, we will need to see your weapon."

"You and your four soldiers may do what you like," Peyton replied, speaking in a tone that was deliberate. "However, you will have to give me a moment to find my axe. It has been many hours since I had it out, and I am not sure where in the wagon I last placed it."

Edlyn heard him begin to rustle around near the front of the wagon, moving slowly as if stalling for time.

"Hurry up. We do not have all night," a different solider snapped.

Edlyn carefully wrapped her hand around the axe and slid it underneath the edge of her skirt so it was out of sight.

"Peyton, this is taking far too long. What is the matter?" Briac snapped.

"It was a busy morning as you can imagine, sir. I am not sure where I placed my weapon."

"Then we shall just have to help you," Briac replied. "Men, search the wagon!"

Edlyn heard the other men approaching.

"I ask that you be careful of the plants," Peyton quickly called out. "The king and queen expect them to arrive in good condition, of course."

"Of course," Briac replied with a cough. "We do not want to damage the delivery."

As the soldiers reached the wagon, Edlyn caught her breath and shut her eyes. An instant later, the blanket over her was torn off.

"Please," came Peyton's voice, "have respect for the dead."

The commotion around the wagon came to a hush.

"I shall take care of the corpse," Briac announced guardedly. "The rest of you, search the remainder of this wagon."

Around her, Edlyn heard soldiers removing the bags of plants from the back of the wagon. Exposed, motionless, and surrounded by Briac's men, Edlyn fought the growing need for air. She then sensed someone come up to her, and the same smell of leather drifted to her nose. It was Briac.

Peyton spoke up, "Sir, I remind you that this is the body of the recently deceased."

"Very well. I shall allow you do the search of her," Briac conceded.

"What?"

"You shall do the search, Peyton," Briac told him again.

Edlyn's lungs burned. Her body was desperate to move. More torturous seconds passed.

"Peyton, why do you hesitate? Surely you want to be on your way as much as I do," Briac's tone was suspicious. "After all, if you are innocent, you have a delivery to make, and I have a murderer to hunt for."

"Very well, Briac," Peyton finally replied. "You leave me no choice."

Peyton's footsteps came right up to the wagon. Edlyn felt his hand come down on top of hers.

"Are you ready?" Peyton asked.

Edlyn realized that his question was directed at her. She felt a lump in her throat and barely moved a finger in reply.

"What?" Briac called out at the same time. "Of course I am ready."

Edlyn felt Peyton slide his hand off of hers and onto his axe, which was still concealed under the edge of her skirt.

"There are two soldiers on the far side of the wagon," Peyton whispered. "Each of them is armed with a sword."

Briac snapped, "What did you say?"

Peyton ignored Briac and continued muttering to Edlyn, "Briac and the two other soldiers are behind me."

Edlyn moved her fingers slightly again, telling Peyton that she had understood.

"Peyton, I demand that you explain what is going on," Briac commanded.

Taking a firm grip of his axe, Peyton said to Edlyn, "On my count, roll to your right and stay down."

From behind Peyton, there came the sound of a sword being unsheathed.

"Peyton, put up your hands," Briac ordered.

"Three. Two," Peyton counted. "One. Now!"

Taking a gasping breath of air, Edlyn rolled to her right until she hit the side of the wagon. The soldiers shouted in alarm and surprise. A horse let out a startled cry. Dogs began barking viciously.

"Capture them!" Briac ordered.

Chaos ensued. Soldiers charged toward the wagon from both sides. Stiff and still partially numb, Edlyn barely managed to turn her head to see Peyton throw his axe. The weapon flew over the wagon, striking a soldier who was attacking from the right. Peyton next rammed his shoulders into a soldier who was coming up behind him. As the second solider dropped to the ground, Peyton pried the sword from his hands.

The wagon rocked. Edlyn screamed as yet another soldier reached over the side to grab her. Mustering all her strength, Edlyn swung her legs, striking him in the face. The soldier let out a screech. Edlyn took her chance, crawling out of the wagon to get away. She ran clumsily for the body of the first solider, pried Peyton's axe from his chest, and snatched up his sword. Her arms and legs tingling painfully, Edlyn turned. The wounded soldier was coming for her, gripping his broken nose. Over his shoulder, Edlyn spotted Peyton fighting both Briac and the last solider.

"Come now, girl," growled the soldier with the broken nose. "We both know that you cannot fight. Surrender now, and you will not get hurt."

Edlyn adjusted the weapons in her hands. As the soldier leapt forward to grab her, Edlyn let out a fierce yell and swung the sword into him. The solider collapsed to the ground, writhing. Edlyn darted past him and ran to Peyton.

"Peyton! Here!" she screamed, holding out his axe.

Peyton extended his free arm and took his weapon from her hands. "Now get back!" he yelled.

Edlyn heard someone running up from behind her. Before she could ready herself, the soldier with the broken nose shoved her forward to the dirt. Peyton attempted to come to her aid, but Briac and the last solider leapt in, stopping him. Peyton shouted furiously and threw his axe, killing the last soldier instantly. Peyton again lunged for Edlyn, but Briac charged forward, keeping him in battle.

Still on the ground, Edlyn struggled to free herself from the soldier's grip. He knocked the sword away from her hand, rolled Edlyn onto her back, and glared down at her.

"You should have surrendered when you had the chance," he seethed.

Just as the soldier raised his arm to strike her, someone else pounced on top of him. Edlyn scrambled to her feet, watching as the new figure raised a dagger, which he drove into the soldier's side. Edlyn let out a cry:

"Maddock!"

Maddock pushed himself to his feet and sprinted to help Peyton, who remained in a fight with Briac.

"Stay back!" Peyton shouted when he saw Maddock coming. "This one is mine!"

Maddock stopped yet kept his dagger ready. Edlyn ran to Maddock's side, watching as Peyton and Briac circled one another with weapons raised. But when Briac noticed Maddock with Edlyn, he did a double take and his eyes widened.

"You are the two peasants. You are wanted by the king and queen," Briac stated, growing pale.

Maddock stepped in front of Edlyn. "She is innocent."

Collecting himself, Briac pushed his curly hair from his face and turned to Peyton once again. "You are the taller and stronger of us, and now you have me outnumbered. I shall most likely die tonight, but as you appear no younger than me, I shall not die without a fight first."

Rather than preparing himself, however, Peyton only pointed his free hand at the soldiers' barking dogs. The animals immediately calmed and sat down. Peyton then spoke to the deputy once more:

"I have no desire to kill you, Briac. However, I am sure you understand that we cannot let you go. You know too much."

Briac lifted his sword. "Then we fight."

"No, you shall cease this immediately," Edlyn ordered, stepping right up to them. "Briac, neither Peyton nor his mother knew who we were when we came to them for shelter. Peyton is innocent. Please let him go his way."

Briac laughed oddly. "You say that Peyton is innocent, and the young man who holds a dagger in his hand insisted that you are innocent." He focused on

Maddock. "So the guilty party must be you, for no one seems to have anything to say in your defense. What have you done to cause so much havoc?"

Maddock shrugged slightly. "I am from the Colleland. I am trying to break into the castle. I have fought Sheriff Hurst, resisted arrest, killed soldiers, and prevented the sheriff himself from obtaining something—rather, someone—he desires. So choose your reason. There are many to explain why I am wanted."

Briac's mouth fell open.

"Now," Maddock went on, putting his dagger away, "as you have already acknowledged, you have no chance of escape or survival. So what are you going to do?"

Briac looked helplessly between the others. "I work for Sheriff Hurst...for the king and queen. I have no choice but to obey orders."

Peyton gestured to his axe. "Briac, be reasonable. You do not want to die, do you?"

"Of course not. I have a wife. I have a child. I—"

"Then do not be a fool," Maddock interrupted. "We are offering you your freedom. All we ask is that you swear never to reveal what you know. Then we will go our way and you can go yours."

Briac smiled despairingly. "It is not that simple. I cannot make an oath to you, for I am already bound by the oath that I made to serve the king and queen. I have sworn to fulfill their orders, even if I must meet my death in doing so."

"Briac," Maddock spoke deliberately, "do you even know whom you swore to serve? Have you met the king and queen? Spoken to them? Seen their faces?"

Slowly, Briac shook his head. "No, but only a very select few have ever seen the king or queen."

"That is true, Briac," Maddock agreed. "Only a very few know the real identity of those who rule over this kingdom...because Guthrie and Raelin make sure that the people of Nereth are kept in ignorance."

Brian seemed almost offended. "Are you trying to suggest that the Guthrie and Raelin of ancient legend continue to rule over Nereth today? Do you think I am fool enough to believe that?"

Maddock was about to answer when Peyton stepped forward.

"So the stories really are true, Maddock?" Peyton asked him quietly. "Guthrie and Raelin reign over the kingdom even now?"

Maddock nodded. "Yes. It has to be so."

Briac scoffed. "You two cannot expect me to believe that the children of King Whittemoor are still alive. Come, stop playing games with me, gentlemen. I will not let you mock me any longer. Peyton, let us fight and finish this."

"But it is true, Briac," Edlyn insisted. "You must trust us."

"Trust you?" Briac repeated. "Trust the young woman who pretended to be a corpse? Trust the man who killed my soldiers? Trust the outlaw who claims to be from the Colleland? How can you possibly expect me to trust anything that you say?"

Edlyn looked to the others for help. In response, Maddock began walking closer to Briac. The deputy made a cry and prepared to swing his sword. Without flinching, Maddock only pulled back his left sleeve, revealing the symbol of the Colleland on his shoulder.

"Yes, Briac, we are asking you to trust us," Maddock said.

Briac dropped his sword. "Then the legend is real," he uttered in amazement, "and you are the one who has come to save our land."

"Yes, the legend is real." Maddock pulled his sleeve down. "But I am not the one of whom the ancient stories are told. I am only here to save a friend who was wrongly imprisoned. I swear that is all."

Briac was silent for a long time. He finally turned to Peyton. "And what is your story?"

"I work for the king and queen so that my mother and I might keep our farm," Peyton answered. "Nothing more."

Lastly, Briac peered over at Edlyn. "And how, young lady, did you get involved in all of this?"

"Stubbornness," Edlyn remarked. "Or fate. Perhaps both."

Maddock glanced at her, and Edlyn gave him a small smile in return.

Briac again looked between the three of them and then started pacing. "So what am I to do? I cannot serve such evil tyrants as Guthrie and Raelin. I would never have taken an oath had I known whom I was vowing to serve. I am left with no choice but to abandon my oath and die in dishonor."

"Briac, you are bound by nothing," Maddock spoke firmly. "The oath that you made is meaningless."

Briac paused as if waiting—hoping—for Maddock to go on.

"Sheriff Hurst lied when he hid the true identities of those you were agreeing to serve." Maddock shook his head. "And an oath that is not made in complete honesty is no oath at all. There is nothing that binds you, and you owe no one your service. Your honor remains intact."

Briac's breathing became strong, and new life appeared in his eyes. "Then tell me: what can I do to help you?"

"Much," Maddock replied, extending his arm. "You will be a valued ally and a friend."

"Thank you. We are at peace," Briac said sincerely, shaking Maddock's hand. He then looked to Peyton. "Peyton, we are at peace."

"Yes." Peyton clasped the hand that Briac offered. "We are at peace."

Briac then faced Edlyn. He held out his arm. "Young lady, it will be a privilege to help you. We are at peace."

"Thank you, Briac. We are at peace," Edlyn replied, and she reached out and shook his hand.

After a few moments, Maddock spoke once more, "Forgive me, but we can delay here no longer. We have a long way to travel before this night is through."

"Yes," Briac replied with a slight bow. "We shall depart."

With a content smile, Edlyn turned and began walking toward the wagon. She heard footsteps coming up behind her. She knew it was Maddock, but she ignored him and kept going.

"Edlyn, what were you thinking, sneaking away in Peyton's wagon like that?"she heard Maddock say. "Had you reached the castle, you would have been captured or even killed. Why did you not stay with Vanora?"

Edlyn spun around. "What were *you* thinking, Maddock? You left without even saying goodbye."

"I was doing the right thing."

"The right thing?" Edlyn repeated. "You abandoned me, Maddock. How is that the right thing?"

"Edlyn, I—"

"Do you have any idea how hurt I was? Far more importantly, do you have idea how worried I was about you? I was left knowing that you were heading alone into unspeakable danger. Do you not understand?"

Maddock came to a stop in front of her, his expression steady. "I do understand, Edlyn. I understand that I left you in the care of someone who could finish nursing you back to health. I understand that I left you somewhere safe while I did everything in my power to stop Sheriff Hurst from ever hurting you again." He looked away. "I understand that I left so, one day, you might recognize there is a good man who clearly cares for you—a man who is not a wanderer or an outlaw—a man who would give you security, love, and happiness, if you wanted to be with him."

Edlyn followed Maddock's gaze and swallowed hard. He was watching Peyton, who was gathering up his supplies.

"Edlyn, I did what I believed was best for you," Maddock went on simply. "I was not able to say goodbye."

Edlyn's heart swelled. She longed to tell Maddock how she felt—something she was only truly coming to understand herself—but she did not. Instead, Edlyn stepped back from him and remarked:

"You were foolish to think that I would simply stay behind when I realized you were gone."

"That is why I slowed my pace when night fell. When the storm cleared, I knew that Peyton would be departing for the castle. I figured that I should keep watch, in case you tried to join him." He grinned a little. "I did not, however, expect you to surprise him the way that you did."

Edlyn smiled.

"We are almost ready to depart," Peyton called.

Edlyn and Maddock looked over at him. Peyton had finished securing the supplies and preparing his team of horses. Nearby, Briac was holding the soldiers' horses by the reins and keeping the dogs at his heels.

Maddock spoke once more to Edlyn, "There is still time to take you back to Vanora before—"

"Before what?"

"Before I finish what I came here to do. Alone."

"No, Maddock, I shall not go back," she replied with gentle firmness. "I believe that there is a reason our paths crossed. I believe that I am supposed to join you on this journey."

Maddock was quiet for a long time, and then he reached out and took her hand. "Very well, Edlyn. It is time to see what our journey has in store."

12

Only the brightest stars were still visible in the early morning light when Peyton brought his wagon to a halt at the river's edge. "I do not know how you two survived this," he remarked to Edlyn and Maddock, watching the water flow swiftly past.

From atop the horse she rode, Edlyn remained silent. She saw a few remnants of the destroyed bridge washed up on the riverbank, but everything else had been swept away in the storm.

"We survived, thankfully, because one of the two of us can swim," Maddock quipped, adjusting his grip on his horse's reins.

Peyton raised an eyebrow and peered over at Edlyn.

"I did not believe him at first, either," Edlyn remarked with a grin, reading Peyton's thoughts. "But it is true—while he knows a great many things, Maddock does not know how to swim."

Maddock only shrugged.

Briac rode up, leading the other horses, with the dogs following closely behind. "The river is deep and the current fast. With the bridge gone, how are we going to cross?"

Peyton's face resumed its typical solemn expression as he gestured to the south. "There is another bridge past the bend. I have used it when my wagon load was too much for the bridge that used to be here."

"If we take that route, we shall have to backtrack quite a distance once we are on the western shore before reaching the castle," Briac noted worriedly. "We will lose time."

"Unfortunately, we do not have any other choice," Peyton replied. "It is the only way to get the wagon across."

Maddock studied the sky. "The night is waning. We need to hurry. Is everyone ready?"

At his words, the mood among the group instantly changed.

Briac spoke first, quiet though resolute, "Yes, Maddock, I am ready."

Peyton gave Maddock a nod. "I, too, am ready. Let us finish this."

Maddock slowly—almost reluctantly—turned to Edlyn.

"I am ready, of course," she told him. "I am ready to go with you."

Maddock took a deep breath. "Very well. We all know the plan, so let us be off."

Maddock dismounted his horse and helped Edlyn off hers, and then he handed both of the animals' reins to Briac. "Travel safely to the castle, friend," Maddock told the deputy. "We shall not be far behind you."

***

Peyton made a call to his team of horses. When the wagon came to a stop, Peyton dropped down from his seat and walked to the back.

"Daylight is appearing," he whispered. "We are near the edge of Ravenshire Forest, on the road that leads to the castle gates. We are almost there."

Hidden in the back of the wagon beside Maddock, Edlyn shivered as Peyton's words reached her ears. For the first time since they had ventured down the mountainside, the magnitude of what they were about to do struck her fully. She found herself growing truly and terribly afraid.

"And Briac?" Maddock asked in a hushed tone.

Peyton bent closer to the wagon and continued speaking under his breath, "He kept a reasonable distance ahead of us. No suspicion was drawn. He crossed the drawbridge with the soldiers' horses and dogs, and he has just passed through the castle gates."

"Then we shall soon know whether or not Sheriff Hurst believes his story," Maddock noted tensely.

The discussion was interrupted by a familiar voice:

"You use a rather strange way to travel, Fugitive."

Edlyn let out a gasp of joy. "Kegan!"

At the same moment, Peyton made a startled grunt. "Who are you, little man?"

"I beg your pardon," Kegan retorted indignantly, "but I am not a little man as you so rudely—"

"Forgive him, Kegan. We are all a bit uneasy," Maddock called out from his hiding place with a hint of amusement. "And do not worry, Peyton, the Langerlan is our friend."

"A Langerlan?" Peyton sounded stunned.

Kegan went on, "Yes, but given what you appear to be doing, proper introductions shall have to wait. Large Man, bring your wagon and its concealed occupants into the shelter of the forest. And move quickly. You will be spotted if you foolishly remain out in the open like this."

Peyton's footsteps could be heard hurrying to the front of the wagon. He climbed into his seat and snapped the reins. The wagon began rolling. Soon, the heat of the overhead sun disappeared, replaced by a cool, misty dampness. Trees far above rustled in the wind as the wagon traveled farther into Ravenshire Forest.

"Whoa," Peyton told his horses, bringing the wagon to a rest.

"My friends, you are safe to come out of your hiding place," Kegan announced. "I have positioned Langerlen all about, and they will sound a warning if anything suspicious is sighted. However, I doubt we will have much to worry about in the forest today. There has been unusual excitement at the castle, which continues to keep Sherriff Hurst and the soldiers quite occupied."

Peyton leapt from his seat and took off the cover that hung over the wagon. He moved aside bags of plants and herbs that were in the back, and then he lifted the blanket underneath, exposing where Maddock and Edlyn were hidden.

"Are you two alright?" Peyton asked, observing them.

Edlyn sat, stretched, and breathed in the fresh air. "Yes, although this reprieve is most welcome." She looked over the side of the wagon and smiled down at the Langerlan. "It is very good to see you again, Kegan."

"It is good to see you, too," Kegan replied sincerely, giving her a bow. He peered at Maddock. "It is also nice to see you, Fugitive, as stubborn and hard-headed as you are."

"Why, thank you, Kegan," Maddock replied, the corners of his mouth twitching slightly.

Kegan let out a sigh. "Indeed, it is a joy to be reunited. We Langerlen have been profoundly worried about your welfare. Long days and nights have been spent watching and hoping that you two survived after the bridge went down during the storm."

"We certainly have had more than a few close calls since we departed the forest last," admitted Edlyn.

Maddock slid forward and climbed out of the wagon. "Kegan, how did you know that Edlyn and I were hiding in here? We thought that we were well-concealed."

"You were very well-concealed, Fugitive. Discovering you was a most unexpected, wonderful find," the Langerlan informed him. "I did not know what this wagon carried when it first came into view, but as I watched from the forest, I quickly realized that something was amiss." The Langerlan gestured to Peyton. "We have often seen Large Man come to the castle with his deliveries over the years, but never before has he stopped on the road to adjust his load. Nor has his wagon ever been so full. And he most definitely has never talked to his supplies before."

Peyton scratched his head. "Apparently, I was not as subtle as I hoped."

"It is hard to get anything past the Langerlen," Edlyn laughed. "Worry not, Peyton, you have been doing admirably. We would not be here at all, were it not for you."

The slightest hint of color came to Peyton's cheeks under her praise. He shifted so that he was facing the other way.

"Yes, we keep a sharp watch over this forest," Kegan stated, puffing out his chest proudly. "As I said, Large Man's behavior was a bit unusual. So with my curiosity piqued, I moved in closer to investigate why he was speaking to his wagon in such a manner. It soon became clear that he was transporting something far more significant than supplies. To my immense happiness, the voice that I heard speaking back to him was one I recognized as belonging to a certain obstinate young man."

Edlyn laughed again and moved to climb down from the wagon. Both Maddock and Peyton extended a hand to help her. Edlyn hesitated, glancing uncertainly between them, until Maddock dropped his arm. Slowly, Edlyn put her hand in Peyton's, letting him assist her to the ground. Peyton then quickly let her go, saying nothing. Edlyn made herself busy straightening out the skirt of her dress.

"Maddock, we welcome you and your companions into the shelter of Ravenshire Forest," said a voice from the trees. "It seems that fate wants your quest to continue."

The group spun around. Ailith was appearing out of the darkness.

Maddock nodded to her. "Yes, Ailith. Fate or otherwise, I am here to finish what I set out to do."

Ailith glided toward him. "Then may that which brought you here continue guiding you safely, until your quest is complete." She turned to Edlyn, and her eyes clouded with grief. "Your journey has not been an easy one, Edlyn, but you have borne it bravely."

"I can take no praise, Ailith, for this has not been an easy path for any of us," Edlyn explained. "I am here only because of the help of others."

"Indeed," Ailith remarked. She gestured to Peyton. "You, Peyton, are one who has given the help that was so needed."

Peyton only gawked, rendered speechless.

"Forgive me," Edlyn spoke up to the Langerlen, her face reddening, "but although I embarrassed myself once before in this manner, I must do as counseled. I seek to know that you...are who you say you are."

"You are wise, Edlyn," Kegan commented, rolling up his sleeve to show her the symbol on his shoulder.

"Yes," Ailith agreed, revealing her mark as well. "You are wise, indeed."

"What is this?" Peyton whispered, finding his voice. "You are marked? It is a symbol much like the one that was on the shoulder of my late father."

It was Maddock's turn to be stunned. "Peyton, your father was from the Colleland?"

Peyton looked directly at him. "Yes. My father found and entered the Kingdom of Nereth, Maddock, just like you."

Maddock breathed out slowly, fell into silence, and looked away, appearing deep in thought.

Kegan stepped forward. "It is clear that I owe you an apology, Edlyn," began the Langerlan humbly. "I did not think you could be correct when you insisted that another from the Colleland had walked in Nereth. I was mistaken. I am sorry."

Edlyn bent down and put a hand on Kegan's shoulder. "You have nothing to apologize for. Had I not seen him myself when I was young, I would not have believed, either."

"And you seek him still," Ailith added, studying her.

Edlyn met the Langerlan woman's penetrating gaze. "Yes, Ailith. I vowed to find that man, and I shall not rest until I do so."

"Many have a quest in this life." Ailith's eyes shone. "It seems that fate has given you yours."

"I do not know if fate has anything to do with it, for what I have vowed is nothing noble," Edlyn stated frankly. "Yet it is my mission nonetheless, and I intend to see it through."

The trees swayed again in the wind, but the peaceful sound was interrupted by unexpected music in the distance.

Maddock looked in the direction of the castle. "That was a trumpet call."

"Yes. Such commotion has been going on at the castle all morning," Kegan relayed. "Trumpets, crowds, dancing, carriages, nobility, decorations, soldiers...the festivities are unlike anything I have seen at the castle for centuries."

Edlyn did not hide her worry. "With everything that is going on at the castle today, how will we ever discern a sign from Briac?"

Kegan faced her with interest. "A sign?"

"We have been fortunate enough to gain the friendship of one who works within the castle gates," Edlyn explained.

Maddock added, "And we can only hope that Briac will remain safe as he attempts to assist us."

"What is the sign that you await? I will tell the other Langerlen to keep watch," Kegan offered.

"We do not know," Peyton said.

Kegan tipped his head and blinked at him. "You do not know? What kind of a sign is that, Large Man?"

"Briac promised to give us any sign that he could. If he could," Maddock interjected. "A sign from Briac will mean that the sheriff believed his alibi, and that Briac can position himself at the castle gates to assist with smuggling Edlyn and me inside."

Kegan appeared intrigued. "And what is the alibi that Briac will tell the sheriff?"

"That he and his four soldiers were attacked by a young man in the eastern hills last night," Maddock answered, "and Briac was the only survivor."

"Your friend is going to claim that he lost a battle when he had a five-to-one advantage?" Kegan smacked his lips doubtfully. "How do you know that the sheriff will believe such an unlikely tale?"

"We do not know," Maddock acknowledged. "I am gambling on emotion—that when Sheriff Hurst hears Briac's story, he will realize I must still be alive, and his anger will cloud any rational thinking that would otherwise make him question Briac's tale."

Another trumpet call carried through the forest.

Maddock turned again toward the sound, shifting uneasily. "What is the cause for such celebration at the castle today?"

"We do not yet know," Kegan spoke disappointedly. "We Langerlen have had to move with extra caution due to the number of people traveling along the road near the forest today. Our ability to gather information has been hampered greatly."

"This is unfortunate timing," Peyton muttered. "Even if we do receive Briac's sign, the castle grounds will be filled with courtiers, royalty, entertainers, and extra soldiers. Our task will be made far more difficult."

"Perhaps the commotion will prove to be to our advantage," Edlyn tried sounding optimistic. "The crowds might provide us anonymity that we would not have had otherwise."

Yet another trumpet call filled the air.

Maddock suddenly whipped around. "I need to see the castle gates."

Edlyn stared at him, alarmed by his tone. "Maddock? What is wrong?"

"This is too unusual." Maddock paced. "What is taking place at the castle cannot be coincidence."

"Say no more, Fugitive." Kegan was already moving deeper into the trees. "Follow me to the watchtower, everyone."

Kegan hurried off with Ailith close behind him. The others exchanged looks and rushed to follow, however the light-footed Langerlen were soon far ahead and gone from sight. When the humans finally reached a clearing, they found Kegan and Ailith waiting beside a massive, ancient tree.

"From our watchtower, you will safely be able to await the sign from your friend," Kegan told them.

Edlyn was bewildered. They had been led deep into the forest, where no view of the castle was possible. She stayed silent, though, curious and waiting.

Kegan reached out and rested his palm on the trunk of the tree. To Edlyn's amazement, the tree started to emit a faint glow, which brightened and expanded until the entire tree had become enveloped by a swirling green light.

"Enter, Maddock," Ailith said to him.

Maddock's expression of uncertainty changed to one of understanding. He went right up to the tree until he could go no farther. But then he somehow took another step forward, disappearing inside.

Edlyn's jaw dropped.

Keeping his hand on the tree, Kegan addressed Peyton, "You are next, Large Man."

Peyton hesitated for only a moment before he approached. Like Maddock, he reached the tree, somehow took another step, and was gone.

"Now you, Edlyn," Kegan invited her. "Enter, and we shall be behind you."

Edlyn gently fingered her necklace, which seemed to calm her trembling heart. Then, with deliberate strides, she advanced to the tree. She reached out a hand, exclaiming with wonderment when it became lost from view inside the trunk. She quickly pulled her hand back and stared at it for a few seconds. Then, with a deep breath, she went forward. There was a rush of warmth. All was still. Edlyn opened her eyes.

She found herself standing inside a circular room, which was dark except for daylight streaming in through a large, shimmering window opposite her—a window that gave no reflection of Peyton and Maddock, who were standing before it.

"Come, Edlyn. Come see," Maddock said, sounding awed.

As Edlyn joined the others, Maddock tapped on the window, causing it to ripple like liquid. Edlyn watched, fascinated, until the last ripple died away. She then stepped right up to the window and looked out, shocked by the sight that met her eyes.

Incredibly, the room was high in the air, and the window provided them an unobstructed view beyond the forest. Far below, they could see the dusty road that they had so recently traveled. The road was bustling with carriages and people on foot, all heading for the drawbridge that crossed a wide moat to the castle gates. The massive gates were open, revealing a partial view of a vast courtyard on the other side. At the far end of the courtyard stood the castle itself. Cold and ominous, the castle's spires and towers seemed to stretch upward forever.

"Oh, Maddock," Edlyn sighed, "how will you ever find Ronan in there?"

From the expression on his face, Maddock seemed to be wondering the same thing. "I do not know, Edlyn. I do not know."

Edlyn resumed watching out the window, fear rising anew within her. The only way into the castle grounds was to go through the gates, passing the armed soldiers who were screening every person and searching each carriage. If they actually made it beyond the gates, more soldiers were patrolling inside with weapons ready. And even if they managed not to arouse the soldiers' suspicions, they still had to get inside the castle itself to find the prison, where surely Raelin and Guthrie—and other horrors not yet known—would be waiting.

It would be a miracle if they survived.

"Well, if there is anywhere we will be able to see a sign from Briac," Peyton noted, "it is from here."

Maddock replied, "If Briac is alive to give us any sign at all."

Edlyn winced. "You think Sheriff Hurst would kill Briac?"

"For aiding me? And aiding you? Most assuredly."

The three of them fell back into tense silence. Down below, the road leading to the castle remained a parade of activity as fancy carriages and extravagantly dressed people moved past the entertainers and merchants who lined the way. In the courtyard beyond the castle gates, crowds cheered and music played while colorful flags waved in the breeze. Even the sun seemed to be shining more brightly than usual.

Peyton shook his head. "I have never seen the castle grounds this way. It is always dark and quiet. What is taking place today is most unusual."

Maddock's eyes darted over the scene. "Too unusual. It is like Raelin and Guthrie are trying to send a message. Only something extremely significant would prompt them to put on a display of this kind."

"Significant, indeed," they heard Ailith say.

They looked over their shoulders. Ailith and Kegan were behind them.

Maddock gave the Langerlen a nod and turned again to the window. "You say that no one yet knows the reason for all of this?"

"We just received report," Kegan stated somberly. "It is a hanging."

"A hanging?" Edlyn sputtered, horrified.

Maddock slowly faced them again. "Who is to be hung?"

"No one knows his name," Kegan answered, keeping his green eyes meaningfully on Maddock. "They only say that the man is a prisoner who was captured during a sword fight many days ago. A prisoner despised by the king and queen."

"Ronan," Maddock whispered. He swayed slightly, but then his voice became firm, "I must go."

"You cannot go yet," Edlyn protested. "We have not had a sign from Briac. We have no way to enter the castle safely. We had a plan—"

"The plan means nothing now," Maddock declared, his tone hollow.

Peyton stepped forward. "I shall go with you."

"No. Stay here," Maddock told him. "I need you to keep Edlyn safe."

Edlyn angrily threw up her hands. "For the last time, I am not simply going to allow you to decide what—"

"You are not coming, Edlyn," Maddock spoke with calm resolve. "Ronan will die unless I act now. Briac is dead if Sheriff Hurst's suspicions are raised. Peyton and Vanora were already endangered. You have been brought close to death more than once." He shook his head. "I have put far too many people at risk, and I shall not let it go on any longer."

"You cannot go alone!" Edlyn exclaimed.

"She is right. You will need help, Maddock," Peyton told him. "The king and queen are also enemies to me, and I am not afraid to fight them."

Maddock put a hand on his shoulder. "Peyton, you have a mother to care for. I cannot ask you to abandon her. What I do ask is that you make sure Edlyn gets out of here safely. That is the biggest service you could render me. Promise me that you will do this."

"Maddock, stop acting as though I am not here," Edlyn demanded. "I will have a say in my own—"

"Promise me, Peyton," Maddock repeated, ignoring her.

Peyton put his hand firmly on Maddock's shoulder. "I promise you, Maddock."

Maddock did not even glance at Edlyn before he addressed the Langerlen, "I need to go. This is my journey. This is my fate."

Ailith's glowing eyes rested upon him. "Very well, Maddock. Come with me."

She turned, walked toward the back of the room, and was gone. Fingering the dagger at his side, Maddock followed.

"Maddock, wait!" Edlyn called out, lunging after him.

Peyton reached out and held her back. "Edlyn, he has chosen to go alone."

"Get your hands off of me!" Edlyn fought to get loose. "You cannot do this!"

But Peyton did not release her, and when Edlyn again raised her head to the back of the room, Maddock was gone. She let out a cry of despair

"Edlyn, I am sorry," Peyton told her, finally letting her go.

Edlyn sprinted for the back of the room, reaching out wildly. But all she felt was the cold, uneven surface of the wall that blocked her escape. She spun around, putting her eyes on Kegan.

"Kegan, we must go after him."

"Edlyn, the sign from your friend did not come," Kegan said sorrowfully. "Fate has taken Maddock one way and steered your course in another. A Langerlan cannot interfere."

"Cannot interfere? Kegan, you cannot truly believe that," Edlyn's voice shook.

Another trumpet blast filled the air, louder than the last.

"The gates will be closing in fifteen minutes!" came a tense shout from the castle. "All who wish to enter must do so immediately!"

Edlyn caught her breath at the sound of the familiar voice, and she ran to the window. In the distance, she could see Briac standing in front of the castle gates, giving orders to the soldiers.

"It is Briac! He is safe! The sheriff has believed his story! This is our sign!"

Peyton came up behind her. "But it has come too late."

"No, it is not too late," Edlyn proclaimed. "We will not let it be too late, Peyton. Briac has put himself at risk to do this for us, and we are not going to let his efforts be in vain." She looked pleadingly to Kegan. "It is our sign. Whether it is fate or something else that we do not understand, we have been given one last chance. We cannot simply hide here and let it pass. Please."

The Langerlan observed her. Then he bowed. "To the wagon. Follow me."

Kegan evaporated into the blackness. Peyton and Edlyn went after him. When Edlyn reached the back wall, she did not hesitate before continuing to charge forward. The next thing she knew, the cool air of the forest was surrounding her once again. Peyton came to her side, and they saw that Kegan was waiting for them.

"Hurry," the Langerlan instructed with a wave, sprinting off into the forest.

Edlyn and Peyton had to run to keep up with Kegan, who seemed to almost fly over the ground. They retraced their steps to Peyton's wagon and found Ailith standing beside it.

"I sensed you would come, Edlyn," the Langerlan woman told her. "No matter how Maddock tries to prevent it, something continues to bring your paths together."

Edlyn rushed toward her. "Where is he?"

Ailith gestured in the direction of the castle. "He has gone."

In response, Edlyn only climbed into the back of the wagon and curled up as tightly as she could. Peyton hastily began covering her with the blanket, but then he paused and spoke:

"Edlyn, what you said to me about love, happiness, and respect...I want you to know that I think I understand what you mean now."

Edlyn felt a lump in her throat. "Thank you, Peyton. Thank you for everything."

Without saying more, he finished hiding her under the blanket. Edlyn then began feeling the weight of the bags that Peyton started placing on top of her, further concealing her presence. Finally, she heard the cover being put over the back of the wagon, which was followed by the sound of Peyton climbing into the front seat and whistling to his team. The wagon began to roll.

"Farewell, friends. Safe journey," Kegan called out.

"Stay brave," Edlyn was almost sure she heard Ailith say. "The fate of Nereth is in your hands."

13

The cool shade was replaced by the heat of the direct sun as the wagon left the forest and proceeded along the road toward the castle. From her hiding place, Edlyn began hearing people's laughter and excited conversations, passing carriages, music, and calls from merchants who lined the roadway.

"Last call to enter the castle gates!" came Briac's urgent shout from the distance. "Last call!"

Peyton flicked the reins. The horses broke into a gallop, causing Edlyn to be tossed around in the back of the wagon as it picked up speed. There were surprised shouts and exclamations from people on the road as Peyton's wagon flew past them. But onward the wagon charged without slowing until, finally, the rocky terrain underneath its wheels changed to wood. They had reached the drawbridge.

"Stop!" a man shouted.

Peyton brought the wagon to a halt.

"State your name and your business," barked the same man whose voice Edlyn did not recognize.

"My name is Peyton. I am making a delivery to the castle under the orders of Sheriff Hurst," Peyton replied calmly.

The cover over the wagon was thrown back.

"What is all of this?"

"The contents of this shipment are not of your concern...sir. It is a regular delivery for the king and queen."

"I cannot authorize you to enter the castle grounds today," the man snapped. "We are not allowing any unnecessary transactions or deliveries."

"Sir, this is—"

"I said no unnecessary transactions or deliveries. We already have enough to manage in there."

"With all due respect, sir," Peyton continued, "I do not believe that the king or queen would consider this particular delivery unnecessary. They have been expecting this shipment, which was already delayed by the recent storm. I think it would displease them if they had to wait any longer."

"Ah, you think that you know the king and queen's opinions on such matters, do you?" scoffed the man. "Allow me to dispel your misunderstanding. This shipment is not going to enter the castle grounds today. We do not have the time for this, and I assure you that the king and queen will understand."

"Sir, I—"

"The king and queen will not be bothered with shipments from peasants today. Do I make myself clear?"

"You do, sir," Peyton answered. But instead of backing the wagon away, Peyton continued speaking in a way that was pleasant and conversational, "The castle is indeed busy. I have never seen it like this."

"This is the biggest event that Nereth has seen in years," the man explained smugly. "Today, there will be the hanging of a most notorious prisoner."

"Notorious?" Peyton repeated with deliberateness. "What earned the prisoner that distinction?"

"Actually, I do not know." The man hastily cleared his throat. "But no one knows the details, for they are guarded by the upmost secrecy. Security reasons, of course."

"Of course," Peyton repeated. "And you, as part of security, obviously would not know the details about security."

"Yes, I...are you being disrespectful to me, peasant?"

"Not at all, sir. I am merely agreeing that this must be a most unusual event. But I suppose that murdering a man always is," Peyton noted, unfazed.

"Enough, peasant," the man resumed his commanding speech. "I do not have any more time to waste on you. I have told you to be off, so depart."

"Sir, I do not mean to argue with one as important as yourself, however, I again suggest that the king and queen would not want you to delay receipt of this shipment. If you let me inside, I could make my delivery and be gone without getting in anybody's way."

"Peasant, if you do not leave immediately, I shall—"

"Why do you not ask your superior?" Peyton suggested. "Since we are in disagreement, your supervising officer would be the best one to decide, would he not? After all, you do not want to be the cause of upsetting the king and queen if I am wrongly sent away, do you?"

The man seemed to hesitate. "I...very well. Wait here."

Growing hot in her hiding place, Edlyn listened to the man storm off. She stayed still, breathing shallowly and waiting. Long seconds passed before the man's footsteps could be heard returning.

"It is this one here," the man was saying. "He claims to need to enter the castle grounds at once."

A second set of footsteps approached.

"Who are you, did you say?" the second person asked.

Edlyn smiled. It was Briac.

"My name is Peyton. I come from the eastern hills, and I am here to make a delivery for the king and queen," he answered without emotion.

Briac let out an exasperated sigh. "Most inconvenient for you to arrive on a day such as this. But very well. Drive on quickly."

Edlyn's smile disappeared when she sensed a strain in Briac's tone. Peyton seemed to detect it as well, for he immediately flicked the reins and called for his horses to move.

"Wait!"

The other man's shout forced Peyton to bring the wagon to another abrupt stop.

"What is the problem now?" Briac inquired impatiently.

"We have no one available to escort him inside and search the wagon," the man pointed out. "It would be against protocol to allow him to enter without a search. Surely this can wait until tomorrow, can it not?"

"No, this cannot wait," Briac responded, and it was clear that there was more meaning in his words than the other man realized. "This most certainly cannot wait."

Despite the sun overhead, Edlyn's body grew cold. Something was very wrong.

"Sir?" the other man questioned.

"This shipment is something that the king and queen have been waiting for," Briac stated succinctly. "Surely you would not want to upset them."

"Of course not," the man agreed.

"And as our usual personnel for such matters are otherwise occupied, I shall escort this wagon myself."

"You, sir?" the other man was clearly very surprised.

"It will be the most efficient way to take care of this, will it not?" Briac insisted.

"Well, yes, but you are the sheriff's deputy. You should not have to busy yourself with routine—"

"Do you have a better solution?" Briac barked.

"No sir," the man relented. "I am not of the rank to carry out such duties, otherwise I would do it for you."

"So it is settled. Stay here and close the gates as scheduled, and then take your position with the other soldiers. I shall manage this delivery and return shortly." Briac climbed into the wagon and spoke to Peyton, "Hurry on, peasant. If the gates close before your delivery is completed, you will be obligated to stay within the castle grounds until the execution is over."

"I understand," Peyton replied, his words catching just slightly.

The wagon began rolling.

"Drive across the drawbridge to the gates," Briac told Peyton under his breath. Then he raised his voice and shouted, "Make way! Make way!"

There was commotion from all sides as the wagon moved through the crowd that filled the massive drawbridge. The overhead sun disappeared once more, and Edlyn knew that the wagon was rolling underneath the towering archway of the castle gates.

"Once you pass through the gates, do not continue into the courtyard. Turn left and go down the corridor," Briac directed quietly.

Edlyn felt the wagon swing left. Its wheels began rolling over stone as it moved away from the celebratory noise of the courtyard.

"Stop here," Briac said.

Even before the wagon was still, Briac hopped out and rushed farther away on foot. A minute or two passed before the noise of his boots indicated that he was hurrying back.

"I have opened a door ahead. It leads into a tunnel within the wall surrounding the castle grounds." Briac climbed again into the wagon. "Drive there quickly, Peyton."

Peyton made a sound to his horses, and the wagon rolled onward. There was a startling bump, and then everything became damp and dark.

"Wait here while I lock the door behind us," Briac instructed.

Peyton brought the wagon again to a stop. Briac jumped down. Edlyn heard the screech of large hinges, followed by the sound of a metal door clattering shut.

"You made it just in time," Briac stated breathlessly with relief, returning. "I am thankful to have found the three of you before it was too late. Maddock and Edlyn, you may come out. Quickly, though, for I only have moments to tell you what I know before I must return to my station."

Peyton leapt down from his seat, came to the back of the wagon, unburied Edlyn, and helped her to the ground. As her eyes adjusted, Edlyn saw that the wagon had been driven through a tall metal door, which Briac had bolted shut. They were alone in a dark tunnel, which was lit only by the flame of a single torch hanging on the wall. Edlyn could still hear the faint sounds of the celebration outside and the drip of water far off in the blackness.

Briac turned from Edlyn to the wagon and then back to her again. "Where is Maddock?"

"Maddock is not here," Edlyn told him, alarmed by the expression that came over his face. "Maddock left for the castle ahead of us when he learned that it was his friend, Ronan, who was to be executed."

"How did he hear of this?" Briac went pale.

"From the Langerlen," Edlyn answered, and when she saw Briac's shocked look, she rushed to elaborate, "Langerlen are real, Briac. We do not have time to discuss it now, so I will only say that Langerlen reside in Ravenshire Forest, and they have been helping us on this journey." She stared intently at him. "But something is wrong. What is it, Briac?"

"This is all a trap."

"What do you mean?" Peyton demanded.

"A trap to lure Maddock in," Briac finished shakily.

Edlyn's throat went dry.

Briac began wringing his hands. "When I got back to the castle this morning, I found Sheriff Hurst waiting for me. He demanded a report of the night's search and an explanation for why I was so late in returning. I told him my story, certain that he would know it was a lie and imprison me at once. But just as Maddock predicted, the sheriff concluded that Maddock must still be alive and became crazed...almost manic. I have never seen anyone so bent on revenge."

With every word that Briac spoke, Edlyn grew more unsteady. She reached out to Peyton to support herself as Briac continued:

"Once I had told the sheriff my story, he stormed out of the chamber. Where he went, I am not certain, but when he returned, he announced that the king and queen had ordered a trap be laid to capture Maddock. When I asked how this trap was to be accomplished, Sheriff Hurst disclosed to me that they were keeping a secret prisoner in the dungeon. Who the prisoner was, or what he had done to deserve imprisonment, the sheriff would not say. He only said that if we performed a public execution of this prisoner, it would surely lure Maddock out of hiding."

Edlyn staggered. "Maddock is walking right into their trap, exactly as they wanted."

"Then we must figure out a way to let Maddock know what is going on." Peyton's eyes were focused, and he had one hand instinctively placed on his axe. "Briac, what else can you tell us about the events that have taken place at the castle this morning?"

Briac spoke fast, "As soon as the decision was made to set the trap, everything went into motion here at the castle. Construction of the gallows and stands for spectators commenced in the center of the courtyard. Messengers were dispatched throughout the land, announcing the grim event to nobility and peasants alike. Decorations were hung. Musicians were ordered to perform. Everything possible was done to attract attention so Maddock would attempt to rescue his friend."

"We should have known," Peyton growled. "These events are so atypical that our suspicion should have been aroused. How could we have been so blind?"

Edlyn bit her lip. "Even Maddock knew something had to be amiss. Did he not say that the king and queen appeared to be trying to send a message? But we did not have the time to think it through. We did not realize for whom the awful message was intended."

"My friends, I am so very sorry." Briac dropped his head. "I am sorry that I did not find you sooner. I could have prevented you from getting into this danger."

"Briac, you did everything that you possibly could for us, and you risked your own life by doing so," Peyton replied firmly. "You have nothing to apologize for."

From outside, there came another trumpet call.

Edlyn wiped the tears from her eyes. "Briac, when will the execution take place?"

"At five this evening."

She turned to Peyton. "We do not have much time."

"Time? Time to do what?" Briac asked. "Maddock could be anywhere. How will we find him? And even if we do find him, there are soldiers guarding the gates, blocking any chance of escape. Maddock is as good as trapped already. The soldiers have been instructed to sound the alarm when Maddock is sighted. I fear he will not get out of here alive."

There was an unexpected knock on the metal door from the outside.

"Stay here," Briac told the others in a whisper.

Edlyn and Peyton backed out of the torchlight. Briac unbolted the door and swung it open, standing so that he blocked a view of the inside of the tunnel.

"Very good, men," Briac could be heard to say. "I will finish securing the tunnel and be out shortly. What? No, I do not need help. My search is almost done."

Briac hurriedly pushed the door closed and locked it tight. He ran back to the others, speaking in an agitated tone, "Soldiers already patrol outside. If you are seen, Peyton, they will surely wonder why I brought you in here, and they will demand that you be detained and questioned. If they search the wagon, Edlyn will be discovered."

"Which I am sure the sheriff would love," Peyton remarked bitterly with a sideways glance at her. "We shall stay here, but you should go, Briac. Go before you begin drawing suspicion to yourself."

"Yes. Go, Briac," Edlyn agreed, feeling as though her heart would break. "Save yourself."

Briac looked with concern between the two of them. "But what will you do?"

"We will try to find some other way out of here or wait for you to return." Peyton gestured into the darkness. "Where does this tunnel lead?"

Briac seemed despondent. "A dead end. This tunnel runs down the center of the wall that surrounds the castle grounds. It is meant to be a place of hiding during an attack. With the door secured, there is no other way in and no other way out."

Edlyn spun around and peered down the tunnel. "That cannot be. Lord Faddin's manor house had a lot of secret tunnels and passageways, and nothing ever led to a dead end. There must be another way to get out."

Briac was watching her curiously. "As a young boy, I heard it said that there are secret passages within the castle walls, which are guarded by ancient magic. But those are stories that no one speaks of anymore."

Edlyn eyed both of them. "Magic or not, there has to be another way out of here."

"And if there is magic, I certainly hope that it is in our favor," Peyton quipped.

From outside in the courtyard, they could hear another haunting cheer of the growing crowd.

"You should hurry, Briac," Peyton repeated and motioned again to the door. "Return to your duties so Sheriff Hurst does not begin to doubt you."

Briac removed Peyton's team of horses from the wagon. "I shall unlock the castle gates myself and release the animals."

"But the soldiers just outside and at the gates?" Peyton questioned. "What will they think?"

"Nothing of consequence," Briac told him. "This is not the first time that animals have been in lodged in here for safety at one time or another. I will let the horses out, and if Langerlen are real and are watching, they will coax your animals into the protection of the forest."

"They are watching," Edlyn whispered. "I am sure that the Langerlen are watching."

With a last look at the others, Briac moved for the door. "Once I get your horses outside, I will go to my post. I shall do all in my power to get you out of here when this is over. Farewell, friends."

Peyton bowed. "Farewell."

"Thank you, Briac." Edlyn waved sorrowfully.

The deputy again unbolted the door and led the animals through. After the door closed behind him, Peyton and Edlyn could hear the ominous clank as it was secured from the outside.

Quiet followed. Peyton turned to Edlyn. She ignored the concern in his eyes and rushed to the wagon, searching until she found one of the swords that they had brought. Edlyn swiftly slung the sword over her side and then donned a cloak.

"I promised Maddock that I would protect you, Edlyn," she heard Peyton say as he came up behind her. "Even if it meant getting you out of here safely at the expense of his own life."

Edlyn forced herself to keep her voice even, "Do not talk like that. We...we will not have to make that choice."

Peyton did not say more. He stepped to the wall, removed the flickering torch from its mount, and rejoined Edlyn. For a few seconds, they stared into the tunnel's darkness. Then they started walking.

Edlyn gestured to the torch in Peyton's hand. "How long will that last?"

"Not long."

Edlyn reached out as they continued, touching the stone wall on her right. "Another way out," she muttered. "There must be another way out."

Minutes passed. More music and cheering could be heard outside, causing Edlyn and Peyton to pick up their pace. Deeper into the tunnel they ventured while Peyton moved the torch from side-to-side, trying to spot anything that might indicate an exit.

"I do not see a way out," he said after a while.

"This tunnel cannot simply lead to a blind end," Edlyn insisted. "There has to be a reason that this tunnel is here. It has to go somewhere. It has to have a purpose."

"As Briac said, it is meant to be a hiding place during an attack. That is its purpose."

"Even a hiding place would have a secret escape."

More time went by. Out of the corner of her eye, Edlyn saw Peyton glance at her again. She knew what he was thinking, but she acted as though she did not see him.

Soon, the light of the torch revealed a wall directly in front of them, forcing them to stop. Peyton swung the flame around and held it higher, searching for a way to continue onward. But they were at a dead end.

"This is the back of the tunnel. There is no way around," Peyton reported somberly.

Distraught, Edlyn started running both hands over the wall. "That cannot be. This tunnel must keep going."

"Or the story of magic passageways is not true," Peyton suggested gently, holding the torch out to help her see.

Edlyn said nothing and continued scouring the wall. The torchlight dimmed as more precious minutes passed. Finally, Edlyn collapsed against the stones and slid down to the ground.

"We have failed, Peyton."

Peyton placed the torch into a mount. "They have not caught Maddock yet, Edlyn. He is smart. He will not do anything unwise."

Edlyn let out an agitated laugh. "You mean, nothing as unwise as attempting to sneak into the castle alone?"

Peyton's silence seemed only to confirm what Edlyn feared. She clenched her eyes shut, trying to come up with a plan while the sounds of ceremonial music and crowds rang in her ears, but she knew that they were up against the impossible. Numbly, Edlyn lifted her tear-stained face and started watching the shadows of the torchlight flicker on the wall to her left.

Then something caught her eye.

"Peyton," she said, scrambling to her feet. "What is that?"

Before he could answer, Edlyn went to the wall and bent down for a closer look herself, blinking hard to make sure that her eyes were not playing tricks on her. Indeed, it was as she had seen: though faded, a small symbol was carved into one of the stones.

"It is the symbol of the Colleland," Edlyn announced breathlessly, leaning even closer to the stone.

Peyton came to her side. He reached out and touched the charm on her necklace, which had slipped out from underneath the collar of her dress.

"A symbol you wear as well, I see," Peyton observed with distinctness to his tone.

Edlyn stood up straight and looked back at him, not understanding. Noting her confusion, Peyton slipped the necklace off of Edlyn and held it aloft.

"The symbol of the Colleland, Edlyn. You have had it with you this whole time."

Edlyn stared at the necklace, which shimmered in the torchlight, and was struck into a stunned, amazed silence. The emblem that hung from the chain was in the shape of a triangle and ornately marked, just like the symbol of the Colleland.

"I...I never realized," she barely managed to say, overwhelmed. "It was my mother's. I do not know what this means."

Peyton looked from the emblem back to Edlyn, and he respectfully put the chain over her head once more. "But one day, Edlyn, you will understand. I am sure of it."

Edlyn used her shaking hand to slip the necklace under her collar. Trying to calm her racing heart, she raised her eyes to Peyton once more. "Right now, though, we must find Maddock."

After another long look at her, Peyton turned again to the wall. "And how do you suggest we do that?"

Edlyn fell quiet, observing the stone. Then, almost as if guided by an unseen hand, she reached out and pressed her hand upon the symbol. The marked stone slid back into the wall with a scraping noise before coming to an abrupt stop, locking into place.

Peyton peered at Edlyn. "Why did you know to do that?"

"I...I have no idea," she told him, astonished.

A low rumble behind the wall caused Peyton to grab Edlyn by the arm and yank her back. The rumbling grew louder, and the ground started shaking beneath their feet. Then, incredibly, the edges of a door appeared in the stone wall. The door swung inward under its own power, revealing an unlit passageway beyond.

In the astonished quiet that followed, Edlyn and Peyton shared an incredulous glance, and then Edlyn cautiously peeked into the passageway. She saw was a sliver of light far off.

"I see daylight! This leads to an exit, Peyton!"

Peyton ran to the opposite side of the tunnel and grabbed the fading torch. He came back and held the flame into the entrance of the passageway, illuminating the narrow, cobweb-lined path.

"I suppose you are going to say that we should go down there," Peyton remarked.

"Of course. Are you ready?"

He looked down at her. "Are you?"

Edlyn shivered, in spite of herself. "We shall soon find out."

Edlyn stepped into the passageway. Peyton followed and placed the torch into a mount on the wall. As soon as he did so, the stone door behind them swung shut, causing them both to start and spin around. The doorway was gone, and the wall was solid once more.

"Ready or not, I do not think we have any choice now," Peyton stated tensely.

With a nervous nod, Edlyn faced forward and led the way. The sounds of the celebration in the courtyard steadily grew louder as they moved farther down the path. Soon, they could make out that the light ahead came from an archway that led to the sunny courtyard beyond.

Edlyn pulled the hood of her cloak closely over her face. "We should split up."

"No. You are not leaving my sight."

"But if I am seen with you, it might raise questions about what you are doing here, Peyton. They assume that you are here to make your delivery. I do not want you to get in trouble because I am—"

"Edlyn, you are not leaving my sight," he said again.

Edlyn did not reply, for they had reached the end of the passageway. They paused, gazing out at the crowded courtyard beyond.

"If we are asked, you tell them that you are a distant relative on my father's side," Peyton told her in a low voice. "You came with me on my journey to deliver the plants to the castle. Since the gates were closed and we were not allowed to leave, we decided to watch the execution."

Edlyn cringed. "How could anyone want to watch a man be murdered?"

Peyton did not immediately answer. He scanned the courtyard and then spoke again, "Should anything happen, meet me back here in this passageway."

"I understand."

He put a suspicious eye on her. "And do not do anything foolish out there."

She actually smiled. "I will not. I promise."

"Very well. Let us go save Maddock."

They stepped out together from the narrow passageway. Immediately, there was a crumbling sound behind them, which could barely be heard over the commotion of the celebration. Looking back over their shoulders, they saw that the arched entrance into the passageway had disappeared. Peyton muttered something under his breath.

"Now what is our plan?" Edlyn asked, unnerved.

Peyton moved close to her. "The only thing that matters is this: if at any time I tell you to leave, you leave. Run for the gates. If the gates are guarded, you hide in the crowd and flee as soon as you are able to do so. Head for the forest and let the Langerlen aid you."

"But what about you? What if—"

"Promise me that if I tell you to leave, you will go as if your life depended upon it."

"Peyton, that hardly—"

"You must promise me, Edlyn. Just as I promised Maddock that I would do all in my power to protect you."

Edlyn hesitated. "I promise."

14

Edlyn and Peyton merged into the crowd. Keeping her face concealed with the hood of her cloak, Edlyn nervously began surveying their surroundings. The entire courtyard was enclosed by the massive stone wall that protected the castle grounds. At the near end of the courtyard, the gate leading to the outside had been shut and was guarded by soldiers. At the far end of the courtyard stood the castle itself, its doors and windows shut tight.

In sickening contrast to the morbid purpose of the event, the mood about the grounds was of one of grand celebration. People dressed in their finest mingled excitedly. Instrumentalists performed jovial tunes while smells of delicious foods filled the air. Children laughed and chased each other. Decorative banners hung from the wall, and brightly colored flags were waving in the warm breeze.

Hidden well among the masses, Edlyn started following Peyton, who was weaving through the throng. When an armed solider passed, eyeing them sharply, Edlyn flinched and dropped her head, holding her breath until the solider continued on. Then she resumed pressing forward after Peyton.

Eventually, Peyton came to a stop. Edlyn lifted her head and saw that they had reached the center of the courtyard, where a large area had been fenced off and surrounded by tiered seating. The seats were quickly filling with courtiers and other nobles who had come to witness the execution. In front of the seats was a wide space for the peasants to stand and watch the event; the space was already packed with people who were cramming up to the fence and fighting for the best view. Immediately on the other side of the fence, armed soldiers were watching the crowd. Farther behind the soldiers was a sight that made Edlyn's blood run cold: the massive wooden gallows, rising up on four thick posts, awaiting the prisoner to be brought forth.

"Come," Edlyn heard Peyton say.

Guiding her through the standing spectators, Peyton carved a route for them right up to the fence.

"Peyton, there are hundreds—thousands—of people out here," Edlyn remarked worriedly. "How will we possibly find Maddock?"

"We will not find him." Peyton kept an eye on the nearby soldiers. "Maddock will find us."

Another trumpet blast filled the air, shrill and important. The entire crowd came to a hush. Edlyn slid closer to Peyton and waited.

"Ladies and gentlemen," a man called out, "it is five o'clock and time for the festivities to get underway! Please take your seats!"

Following the sound of the voice, Edlyn looked toward the wall behind the gallows. The announcement had come from Briac, who was standing atop the wall, surrounded by a group of stern-appearing soldiers.

At Briac's words, the courtyard again filled with a burst of high-spirited activity as the nobility finished making their way to their seats and the peasants pushed even closer to the fence. Finally, the audience settled into an expectant quiet. The only sound came from the colorful flags, which whipped in the wind. The sun continued beating down, causing women to fan themselves and men to wipe their brows. Meanwhile, soldiers patrolled with weapons ready and eyes sharp.

"Ladies and gentlemen," Briac spoke again, making a broad gesture with his hands, "please welcome the honorable Sheriff Hurst!"

The crowd burst into applause. Trumpets began playing. The main doors of the castle opened, parting just wide enough for someone to walk through. A moment later, Sheriff Hurst strode out into the sunlight, dressed in his finest uniform. Those in the stands rose to their feet, and the entire audience cheered even louder.

"Surely Sheriff Hurst cannot be this beloved!" Edlyn exclaimed, incredulous, as she witnessed the fanfare. "He is known for his cruelty, his violent behavior, and his relentless demands on taxpayers. He is despised throughout the land."

"Despised or not, all in Nereth want to be in his good graces," Peyton remarked over commotion. "They whom the sheriff likes receive his favors, including a reprieve from taxes. People are willing to do whatever they must—even pretend to support someone they despise—to gain such an advantage."

Edlyn shook her head, disgusted. "Taxing the people nearly into starvation is a pathetic way to make them cheer for you."

Peyton peered at her. "Yes. This land needs its true leader now more than ever."

Sheriff Hurst came near, staying behind the fence while waving and bowing to the masses with exaggerated graciousness. Edlyn shrank back and ducked her head, hiding from his view. Sheriff Hurst gave the audience another bow and then, accompanied by soldiers, walked to a throne-like chair at the base of the gallows. Once he was in place, Sheriff Hurst made a last appreciative wave before gesturing for those in the stands to take their seats.

Briac addressed the people once more, "Now, ladies and gentlemen, show your reverence for our king and queen!"

Briac motioned again to the castle doors. An eager, palpable stillness settled upon the audience as everyone turned to the castle. But the doors shut. A disappointed, confused murmur began passing through the crowd.

"What is going on?" Edlyn whispered.

Peyton only shook his head.

There was a shout as someone in the audience pointed to the balcony above the castle doors. Others began to do the same. The crowd's murmuring turned into thrilled exclamations as the curtains hanging over the recessed archway behind the balcony were drawn back. A man and a woman stepped out, and the crowd exploded into elated shouts.

"They do not look bad for being hundreds of years old," Peyton remarked sarcastically.

Edlyn was totally bewildered. Standing on the balcony, waving politely to the citizens of Nereth, was an elderly couple that appeared nothing like she imagined Raelin and Guthrie would. The man was short with a large belly. The slender woman beside him was frail and had her gray hair pulled back into a practical bun. Their smiles were warm and their countenances inviting. Were it not for the crowns they wore, Edlyn would have found it impossible to believe that they were a king and queen—and certainly not the evil sorceress and warrior of whom legend was told.

As the applause and music continued, the king and queen kept waving to the people below. Peyton leaned down and whispered in Edlyn's ear:

"They are stalling."

"Stalling? Stalling for what?"

"For Maddock. From the expression on the sheriff's face, I surmise that he does not know where Maddock is yet."

Edlyn shifted her attention back to the chair near the gallows. Sheriff Hurst appeared stiff, his smile gone, as he scanned the crowd. Finally, he looked up at the balcony. The king nodded. Sheriff Hurst bowed and turned toward Briac, who remained on the castle wall above. Briac hesitated for only an instant before raising his arm. Immediately, the soldiers around him stood at attention.

"It is time," Peyton told Edlyn.

Edlyn uneasily put her hand upon the hilt of her sword.

Briac made his next announcement, "Ladies and gentlemen, please take your seats!"

The energy throughout the crowd further increased as everyone obeyed, anticipating what was to come next. Once the people were settled, Sheriff Hurst turned again toward the balcony. The king made a gesture. The sheriff bowed, raised his eyes to Briac, and gave the deputy a signal. A flash of dismay passed through Briac's eyes before he faced the castle and spoke in a loud, commanding tone:

"Soldiers, bring in the prisoner!"

Drums began to be played with a slow, steady beat, and a group of soldiers marched in formation to a wide gate at the base of the castle. The standing crowd began pushing farther forward, and the nobility slid to the edge of their chairs, all straining for a view of what was about to occur. The soldiers reached the gate and pulled it open. From the darkness beyond, two more soldiers emerged, escorting a prisoner between them.

Edlyn's heart pounded when she saw the man who had been condemned to die. The prisoner was tall and strong, with a few streaks of gray in his thick brown hair and beard. His brown eyes were focused straight ahead. He wore a dirtied, ragged shirt, and his pants were torn. He had nothing to cover his feet.

"Ronan," Edlyn whispered.

The crowd, captivated and still, watched as Ronan was led across the courtyard. Drums continued to beat in time with his footsteps, the chilling sound filling the tense quiet.

Edlyn stiffly nudged Peyton. "We must do something."

Peyton's hand had moved to his own weapon. "No. Give Maddock more time."

With a deep breath, Edlyn peered out over the crowd, praying that Maddock was there. Somewhere.

Ronan was brought to the base of the gallows. The drums went silent. Sheriff Hurst rose from his chair and approached the prisoner.

"You have given us no name," the sheriff stated, speaking for all to hear. "You have given us no land of origin. Do you wish to reveal these before you meet your death?"

Ronan did not look at him. He said nothing.

The sheriff threw his head back. "Very well! You are hereby charged with aiding the escape of an outlaw and murdering several of the king's soldiers! Your penalty is death!"

People cheered and shouted mocking insults. The drums beat once more. As the crowd noise swelled, the soldiers grabbed the prisoner by his arms and led him up the steep stairs of the gallows. Once they reached the top, Ronan was made to stand directly behind the noose. Sheriff Hurst climbed the staircase, and then he turned and looked across the courtyard at the gate from which the prisoner had first emerged.

Edlyn leaned out to see what the sheriff was watching for. She shuddered when the executioner appeared. Dressed in all black, the executioner wore a hood so that only his eyes were visible. Whispering spread throughout the audience as the man who would end Ronan's life climbed to the top of the gallows and gave Sheriff Hurst a bow. The drums stopped.

The sheriff faced Ronan once more. "Do you, nameless prisoner, have any last words?"

Ronan finally put his dark eyes upon the sheriff. "Your ploy will not succeed."

Sheriff Hurst seemed startled for only a moment, and then he cleared his throat and put on a smile. "Very odd words for a man about to meet his death. But as you—"

"You will not be able to kill me, Gawain," Ronan interrupted steadily.

Sheriff Hurst's eyes widened. "How do you know my real name?"

"I, like you, am from the Colleland," Ronan replied, his calm voice carrying over the crowd. "The mark on my left shoulder is the same as the one that is upon yours."

There was an immediate, collective gasp from the audience. Sharp muttering escalated into cries of surprise and astonishment.

"Is this true?" one person demanded loudly.

"Sheriff Hurst is a traitor to the descendents of Tiernan!" someone else cried out.

"He has betrayed those from the Colleland!" another voice from the crowd angrily pronounced.

More fervent shouts came from the masses. Sheriff Hurst, visibly stunned, took an unsteady step back from Ronan and wiped his brow. Meanwhile, the increasingly restless crowd started pushing closer to the fence, causing the soldiers to point their weapons warningly. The unrest continued to grow until, from the balcony, the king held up his hand. The people's cries settled into a hush. No one stirred as everyone waited for the king to speak.

"Proceed," was all that the king said.

Murmuring, though more subdued than before, again filtered through the audience. The people turned back to the gallows. Sheriff Hurst stumbled down the staircase, dropped onto his ornate chair, and stared blankly at the ground. It was a while before the sheriff raised his head and made a swift, vehement movement with his arm. In response, the masked executioner put the noose around Ronan's neck and cinched it tight. The two soldiers stepped back. The executioner moved to the lever that would release the trap door beneath Ronan's feet.

Edlyn reached for her weapon. "We must act, Peyton!"

Peyton grabbed her arm. "No, Edlyn. Wait."

Edlyn looked back at the gallows. Ronan had put his eyes directly on the executioner. The executioner reached out to pull the lever.

Edlyn yanked herself free from Peyton's grip. "We have to—"

Someone in the crowd let out a cry. Edlyn whipped her head up. A dagger was flying through the air, which struck the executioner in the chest. The executioner swayed and collapsed. He was dead.

For one moment, all was stunned silence. Then a woman screamed. Others began to yell. Someone in the audience pointed to the castle wall. Edlyn spun around and let out a shout. Maddock, dressed in the uniform of a king's soldier, was standing beside Briac. The other soldiers who had been with the deputy were on the ground. As the audience began crying out in alarm, Maddock grabbed Briac, threw his arm around him, and made a show of holding a sword threateningly against the deputy's neck.

Sheriff Hurst leapt to his feet. "Kill the prisoner! Capture the attacker! Guard the gates!"

More shouts and screams filled the courtyard. Maddock released Briac, grabbed hold of a banner that hung from the castle wall, and used it to slide down into the chaos of the crowd below. People erupted into panicked confusion, while soldiers from all sides began trying to run through the frenzy to capture Maddock.

Edlyn turned back toward the gallows. The two soldiers were rushing for Ronan, whose neck was still cinched in the noose.

"No!" Edlyn exclaimed.

Unseen amid the commotion, Peyton threw his axe. The weapon sliced the rope from which Ronan would be hung and landed at Ronan's feet. Ronan ripped the noose off of his neck, grabbed the axe, and faced the two soldiers, prepared to fight.

Peyton leapt over the fence and bolted for the gallows. With packs of terrified people running past her in all directions, Edlyn gripped her sword and went after him. Up ahead, she saw Peyton ascend the staircase of the gallows, which caused the soldiers at the top to spin around in surprise. Peyton barreled forward and tackled one soldier, tore the sword from his hand, and used the hilt of the sword to knock the soldier unconscious. Meanwhile, Ronan lunged for the other soldier and hurled him off the gallows to the dirt below.

"Peyton!" Edlyn yelled as she rushed up the stairs.

Peyton jerked his head up when he heard Edlyn's voice. "Edlyn! What are you doing?"

"You did not think that I was just going to stand down there and watch, did you?" Edlyn demanded.

Without waiting for Peyton to reply, Edlyn turned. She found herself staring directly up at Ronan.

He studied her with his brown eyes for only a moment, but the power of his gaze struck Edlyn deeply. Then he gestured behind her.

"Here come more soldiers, I am afraid."

Edlyn spun around and prepared her sword. Beside her, Ronan and Peyton traded weapons and also readied themselves. From their vantage point, the three of them watched as the soldiers pushed through the masses below to reach the gallows.

"Kill them! Kill them all!" someone was shouting.

Edlyn looked down and saw Sheriff Hurst hysterically waving his arms, encouraging his soldiers onward through the fray. As he yelled again, the sheriff looked up and stopped short, clearly stunned, when he spotted Edlyn. He called out to his soldiers once more:

"Kill the men, but leave the girl for me!"

The sound of someone rushing up the staircase snapped Edlyn to attention. It was Maddock, carrying a lit torch in his hand. He motioned to the mob of approaching soldiers below.

"It does not appear that the odds are in our favor. I thought this would help."

Maddock held the flame of the torch against the staircase behind him. The wood immediately caught fire and began to burn. People shrieked, backing farther away from the gallows. The soldiers' yells of frustration could be heard as the retreating audience hindered their approach even more.

"Maddock, are you trying to burn us alive up here?" Peyton shouted as the flames grew higher.

Maddock yanked his dagger from the executioner's chest. "Grab the rope and hang on!"

Ronan used both arms to grip the rope that still hung over the trap door. "Come, Edlyn."

Edlyn sheathed her sword and wrapped her arms around Ronan, hanging onto him like a child. Peyton came to her side, used one arm to also grab the rope, and wrapped his other arm around Ronan and Edlyn.

"Ready, Maddock!" Peyton yelled.

Maddock pulled the lever, and the trap door gave way. Peyton, Ronan, and Edlyn fell through the floor of the gallows. Their fall came to a jarring stop an instant later, leaving the three of them dangling a few feet above the ground. Peyton and Ronan released their hold on the rope, and they all dropped to the earth.

"Maddock, come on!" Edlyn screamed up to him.

While flames continued to consume the gallows, Maddock slid down the rope and landed beside them. As soon as his feet touched the ground, Maddock rushed to one of the gallows' four anchoring posts and began ramming his weight against it.

"Help me push!" Maddock cried.

Peyton, Edlyn, and Ronan went to the other posts that held the gallows aloft. With smoke clouding their vision, they pushed together until the wooden posts snapped. The flaming gallows fell, crashing down into the crowd with a tremendous boom. More screams pierced the air as the fire began to spread.

"Come!" Ronan shouted, motioning for the others to follow him. "Hurry!"

Concealed amid the smoke and chaos, the group sprinted across the courtyard. Edlyn realized that Ronan was leading them to the gate at the base of the castle, which still remained open. Before passing through the gate, Edlyn glanced up at the balcony. The king and queen were gone.

A moment later, the four of them made it into the tunnel from which Ronan had originally emerged.

Together, they shut the massive gate behind them, bolting it from the inside.

Lungs burning from the smoke, Edlyn collapsed against the wall, coughing hard and trying to catch her breath.

Maddock came to her side. "Edlyn?"

She looked up at him. "Never...let it be said...that you do not know how to make an entrance...or an exit."

He stopped, and a slight grin appeared on his face. "It is nice to see you, too."

Edlyn began to laugh, until another coughing fit cut her short.

"Here." Peyton held out his flask. "Drink this."

Edlyn took the flask but paused, peering up at him.

"It is only water this time. I promise," Peyton added.

Edlyn smiled and gratefully took a long drink.

"Is everyone alright?" Ronan took a torch from the wall, using the light to observe the others. "Friends, we do not have much time before they will realize where we have gone." He motioned down the tunnel. "This goes to the dungeon, where there is a passageway that leads to the river. If we go quickly, you will be able to escape."

"We will all escape," Maddock pointedly corrected him.

Ronan put a hand on Maddock's shoulder. "My destiny may take me down a different road, but you must leave with your friends, no matter what happens."

"I will not leave without you, Ronan."

Ronan watched his adopted son for a long second before gesturing down the tunnel again. "Follow me and be careful. Danger lurks in every corner of this castle."

Suddenly, the locked gate rattled loudly, and the sounds of angry shouts could be heard outside.

"They figured out where we went," Peyton growled, reaching for his axe.

Ronan held out a hand. "No. This is no place to fight. We must move. Hurry."

While the furious shaking of the gate continued, the group broke into a run. As they raced along the wet floor, the air grew stale and malodorous. Rats scurried past. Cobwebs and decaying skeletons littered the ground. Finally, the tunnel widened, revealing a room lined by empty prison cells.

Ronan pointed to the far end of the dungeon, where the entrance to yet another passageway was barely visible. "That leads to the river! Get out while—"

He was cut off when the prison began shaking violently, as if an earthquake had struck. Edlyn stumbled, fighting to keep her footing. Around her, the prison cell doors swung wildly on their hinges. Torches fell from their mounts, fizzling out in the puddles of water below. Stones started to crumble.

Gripping a wall to brace himself, Maddock used one hand to point at the ceiling. "Move, Peyton!"

Peyton looked up and dove aside just before massive stones from the ceiling crashed down on top of him. Edlyn let out a scream, throwing her arms over her head.

Then the shaking of the ground ceased.

As the dust cleared, Edlyn coughed and dared to look up. "Peyton? Are you alright?"

Peyton, visibly shaken, pulled himself to his feet. "I think so. But I would prefer not to linger here any longer."

Maddock gestured toward the entrance of the passageway. "Unfortunately, it would appear that we need a new means of escape."

Edlyn clapped a hand over her mouth, aghast. The enormous stones that had fallen from the ceiling were piled high in front of the entrance to the passageway. Their escape to the river was blocked.

"Friends," Ronan began tensely, "we are going to have to—"

A howling wind blasted through the dungeon, nearly knocking Edlyn to the ground. The gust blew out the remaining torches, leaving the dungeon in complete blackness. Everything was deathly still.

"What happened?" Edlyn asked feebly.

"It is the queen's magic," Ronan responded in a low voice. "The king and queen must that know we are here."

"How?" Edlyn shuddered, though whether from the chill or fear, she did not know. "How do they know?"

"Perhaps they sensed our presence, or perhaps Sheriff Hurst survived the courtyard fire and alerted them," Ronan answered. "I cannot say."

"Then the time has come at last," Maddock declared. "We must fight them."

Edlyn heard the others ready their weapons. Shaking, she made her way through the dark and joined them. They formed a tight circle, each facing outward, and waited.

The air became ice-cold.

"Do you feel that?" Peyton asked, his voice catching.

No one replied, but Edlyn heard the others adjusting their stances, remaining tensely ready. She clung to her sword and strained her ears to hear, the terrifying anticipation of approaching unknown evil causing her breathing to grow shallow.

From everywhere around them suddenly came the eerie sound of a woman's mocking laugh. The laughter grew louder, echoing off the dungeon walls. The ground trembled once more.

"They have come," Ronan told the others. "Be ready, friends."

Out of the blackness, an iridescent vapor appeared. Edlyn watched with horror as the vapor silently snaked through the air until it surrounded the group. Once they were enveloped, everything again began to quake. Edlyn let out a yell as she felt the floor under her collapsing.

"Edlyn!" Maddock shouted.

She could not reply. The remaining stones beneath her had crumbled away, and she began to fall.

15

The next instant, Edlyn felt solid ground below her feet. There was not a sound. As the glowing vapor cleared, Edlyn spun around fearfully and found that she was alone.

"Maddock! Peyton! Ronan!" she shouted.

Her voice dissolved away into unnerving quiet. As her eyes adjusted, Edlyn saw that she was no longer in the depths of the dungeon; she stood in the center of the great hall of the castle. The room was massive, with gray stone walls and intricately carved archways rising toward the ceiling high above. Torches in ornate mounts flickered, their flames casting shadows into the deeply recessed corners of the room. At the front of the hall, two empty gold thrones sat on a marble platform.

"Hello, Edlyn," someone behind her said.

Edlyn turned, and her entire body jolted from shock. Her father was standing before her.

"I have missed you," he said in a voice that Edlyn had not heard in a very long time and yet was perfectly familiar.

Edlyn reeled. "This is a trick. It is not really you."

"Do you doubt your own eyes?" he asked gently.

Edlyn's voice choked as she replied, "But you...you are *dead*."

He smiled patiently. "Death is only a passage, Edlyn. It is not an ending nor must it be a parting."

"Impossible." She shook her head. "I cannot believe it. I am imagining things, or maybe I am dead, too."

"There is much we assume to be impossible, Edlyn, only because we do not understand it."

Edlyn did not reply. While her mind told her that it could not be true, the person standing before her was indeed her father—in every look, subtle gesture, and inflection of voice. It was he, just as she so vividly remembered him.

"Edlyn?" he asked after a few moments, both with tenderness and concern.

The recognizable way that he said her name caused tears to rise in Edlyn's eyes. Her heart ached, desperate to believe what she saw. Still she resisted.

"It is hard for you to trust," he noted with understanding, as if reading her thoughts.

She spoke cautiously, "Where have you been all this time? Why are you here now?"

"There are ancient powers within these castle walls—powers that allow our worlds to come close. Yet although this is the first time you have seen me with your eyes, Edlyn, I have always been watching over you. I have never been far away."

Edlyn could not help but cry more freely. "There is so much I want to say. To ask."

"But our time together is brief, and there are things we must do."

"Yes. My friends." She hastily brushed tears from her face, collecting herself. "Where are they?"

"I will lead you to them and help you all escape."

Edlyn paused and studied him again. Her heart speeding up, she lowered her sword. "Do you remember my favorite doll? The one with the yellow dress?"

"Yes, I remember the doll very well," he answered with a reminiscent look. "You seemed to always have it with you."

Edlyn broke into a smile. He smiled back and lovingly held out his arms. Edlyn ran toward him. As he moved to embrace her, Edlyn raised her sword and slashed him in the abdomen.

"I never had a doll," she whispered fiercely. "Now tell me, whoever you are, where are my friends?"

He coughed, dropped his head, and went down to his knees, gripping his wound. But he did not bleed.

"Where are my friends?" she repeated with more urgency, holding her sword ready.

When he raised his eyes, it was no longer the pale, stunned face of her father staring up at her. It was Sheriff Hurst.

"Your friends will be dead shortly, for I will kill them, Edlyn, just like I killed your father six years ago."

The revelation struck Edlyn with such force as to render her speechless. Observing her with a malicious smirk, the sheriff got to his feet and removed his arm from his abdomen. He was unharmed.

"After your friends are dead," he went on in his piercing, menacing way, "we will be bound together in a ceremony that will keep you with me forever."

Edlyn swayed as the chilling truth caved in on her fully. For all of those years, she had been in the presence of her father's murderer—the very man she had sworn to kill—and yet she had never known.

The sheriff seemed pleased by her distress. "You must wonder how I could be the man you watched murder your father."

Edlyn gasped.

"Yes, Edlyn, I have always known that you witnessed what happened," Sheriff Hurst said. "I noticed you quivering behind the cabinet on that fateful night. I knew you saw the symbol on my shoulder, but I also realized that my face was not visible. That is why I chose to spare your life."

Edlyn winced, every word he spoke causing her incomprehensible pain.

Sheriff Hurst stepped nearer. "How did I get a mark on my shoulder, you must wonder? Edlyn, I was born in the Colleland. My parents died when I was young, and I was raised by an adoptive family. But I knew that I was destined for better things than farming. Like all in the Colleland, I had heard the legends of Raelin and Guthrie. I was intrigued. I wanted to understand their magic and join them, certain it was my destiny. So I sought out Raelin's spies in the Colleland, and I vowed to them my allegiance. I proved my loyalty by helping them murder many of Tiernan's known or possible descendents."

Chest heavy and struggling to breathe, Edlyn could only shake her head as he continued:

"Once I demonstrated my pledge was true, Raelin's spies guided me to Nereth, where I was soon taken on by King Guthrie himself. In only a few years, I was appointed to be the new sheriff."

"You are a traitor," Edlyn told him through clenched teeth. "You are a coward."

He reached out, putting a hand on her cheek. "I am no coward."

She hatefully pulled her head away. "Do not touch me."

"Edlyn, we cannot continue on like this. We are going to be bound together, and you must learn to love me. If it helps to alleviate your distress, I did not plan on killing your father."

His talking only sickened her more. Edlyn grimaced and bent forward, bracing herself on the hilt of her sword.

"You see, I was also honored by Raelin with the opportunity to return, at times, to the Colleland to act as a spy," he continued to reminisce. "So I walked in disguise among my original people, helping to eliminate any whose heritage might pose a threat to Raelin and Guthrie's rule. In one encounter, however, I was injured. Wounded badly, I returned to Nereth. Too hurt make it back to the castle, I sought help at the manor house of my good friend, Lord Faddin. I did not explain how my injuries were sustained nor did he ask. Loyal friend that he was, he just called to my bedside his best healer: a serf. That serf was your father.

Edlyn shuddered and shut her eyes.

"But, alas, in caring for my wounds, your father discovered the emblem of the Colleland upon my shoulder. I could not have him know my secret, Edlyn. If word got out, I would be labeled a traitor by those in Nereth who secretly—rebelliously—waited for the return of Tiernan's descendent. I might have been attacked or even killed. So once I was strong enough, when your father came to tend to me one night, I murdered him. I am sure you understand that I had no choice."

As the memory of her father's death consumed her mind, fury rose in Edlyn's breast. She let out an enraged cry and rushed Sheriff Hurst, her sword pointed at his throat. But she was not steady, and the sheriff was able to knock Edlyn down and kick her sword from her reach. Edlyn landed on the stone, letting out a sob of rage.

"Edlyn, your actions are pointless." Sheriff Hurst yanked her up from the floor. "The more you fight, the more difficult for you this will be."

"Let go of me!" she screamed, trying to strike him.

The sound of a woman's sinister laughter caused them both to stop. A shiver of dread ran through Edlyn's body as the glowing vapor appeared once again, this time in front of the thrones. Gradually, the vapor brightened and sharpened, morphing into the figures of a man and a woman.

Raelin and Guthrie were before her.

No longer disguised as an aging couple, they stood in their true forms. Raelin was tall, slim, and strikingly beautiful. Her skin was pale. Her black hair was pulled tightly back from her face, revealing her high cheekbones and piercing, light-colored eyes. She wore a shimmering gown and a crown upon her head. Beside her, Guthrie was every bit the warrior that legend had described: dressed in armor, he had fiery red hair, and the same pale skin and light eyes as his sister.

"So this is the girl," Raelin said coldly.

Sheriff Hurst bowed. "Yes, this is she, Your Highness."

"She has caused much trouble," Raelin remarked, observing Edlyn with disdain. "She does not deserve the life of privilege you offer her."

"Life of privilege?" Edlyn glared at the sheriff. "I would rather die than be with you, Sheriff Hurst. You are a pathetic, murderous coward. You are a traitor to the true heir of the throne of Nereth."

Raelin swiftly raised her arm, pointing threateningly at Edlyn. "I would gladly grant your request and kill you right now, girl. However, the sheriff has earned a reward for his valiant service, and he has decided that his reward shall be you."

Sheriff Hurst bowed graciously once more.

"No." Edlyn defiantly threw her head back. "I will not cooperate."

Guthrie chuckled. "She does not seem to appreciate that this is not up to her. It is a respect she will have to learn."

"Indeed." Raelin looked upon Edlyn with hatred. "You are refusing the sheriff?"

"I am refusing the sheriff," Edlyn told her, though she trembled under the queen's glare.

Raelin's eyes flashed. "Then let me convince you to change your mind. I believe that you were accompanied here by some friends, is that correct?"

Edlyn felt a surge of alarm, shrank back, and did not answer.

Raelin seemed to sense that she had found a weak spot. "Yes. Friends you have very strong feelings for. Alas, feelings are dangerous." She laughed, almost pleasantly, and motioned around the great hall. "Your friends have actually been watching us, and I am sure that they are anxious to contribute. I shall remove the spell of silence and invisibility that has been upon them."

"Edlyn!" came Peyton's shout.

Upon hearing his voice, Edlyn had one moment of immense relief. Then she saw him: far to her right, trapped inside of a glowing black cage. Without thinking, Edlyn sprinted across the great hall to the cage, gripped its frigid bars, and shook them as hard as she could.

"Release him!" she yelled over her shoulder to the queen. "He has done no wrong!"

Peyton leaned closer to Edlyn. "It is no use, but do not worry about me. I am not afraid to die. I only regret that I cannot save you first."

"You are not going to die," she declared, still tugging on the bars. "We will get out of here."

"Let her go!" someone else demanded, enraged.

Edlyn's nightmare continued when she heard Maddock's cry ring out. She turned around. On the opposite side of the great hall, Maddock, too, was trapped within a cage. Standing with fists clenched, his furious stare was fixed on Raelin.

Edlyn stumbled toward him. "Maddock, I am sorry. I am so sorry."

He reached through the bars, taking Edlyn's hands. "Do not be sorry. This is my fault."

"This is not your fault," Edlyn insisted, glancing around despairingly, trying to spot anything that could aid an escape. All she saw was her sword, which remained on the ground close to Guthrie and out of reach. Fighting the tightness in her throat, she looked again at Maddock. "We are not going to end our journey like this. Do you hear me? We are going to get out of here. All of us."

"Such a touching reunion," Guthrie snidely interjected.

"A reunion that I am already losing patience for," Raelin muttered. "Now, there is one more member of this party, is there not? I believe we can thank him for this little gathering, for he is the one whom they so foolishly attempted to rescue."

Raelin waved her hand again, and a third cage became visible in the back corner of the great hall. Ronan could be seen standing inside, though his features remained hidden in the shadows.

Raelin put her spiteful gaze back on Edlyn. "Do you still refuse to cooperate with our commands?"

Edlyn did not reply, looking in a panic from one cage to the next, racking her brain for a plan.

Raelin made an annoyed sound. "Apparently, more convincing is in order."

Jolted to fearful attention, Edlyn faced her. "No! Wait! I only—"

But Raelin pointed one hand at Peyton, and to Edlyn's horror, he let out a scream of pain and collapsed.

"No!" Edlyn shrieked. "No more!"

Raelin ignored her, pointing her other hand at Maddock. He immediately dropped to the ground, writhing silently in agony.

"Stop!" Edlyn begged again. "Stop, please! I will do anything!"

Raelin paused, eyeing her. "I could kill them all right now. Slowly. Painfully."

"No!" Edlyn rushed toward the queen. "Please do not hurt them! I will do whatever you ask!"

Raelin's voice was like ice, "Do you vow to comply with Sheriff Hurst's wishes?"

Out of the corner of her eye, Edlyn saw the sheriff slinking toward her. She recoiled and backed up.

"She does not answer you," Guthrie noted to the queen, sounding entertained. "Perhaps she would prefer to let her friends be tortured and killed."

Edlyn made another survey of the great hall in a desperate search for a solution, but a crushing weight was already settling upon her. There was no way out. With a terrible understanding of what she must do to save her friends, Edlyn lowered her head and got to her knees.

"I will obey," she said. "Let my friends go unharmed."

"No, Edlyn!" Maddock shouted. "She is lying to you! She will kill us no matter what!"

"Do not do it, Edlyn!" was Peyton's plea. "Do not destroy your life to save ours!"

Raelin continued watching Edlyn closely. "Do I have your oath?"

"No!" Maddock yelled again.

Edlyn kept her head down. "You have my oath."

Edlyn sensed her tears dry. It was no use fighting any longer. Her fate was decided. Drained of emotion, she did not even resist when Sheriff Hurst pulled her to her feet.

"Let us perform the binding ceremony," Raelin said to the sheriff. She then again addressed Edlyn, "Say farewell to all you know, girl. Once the ceremony is completed, you will be bound to the sheriff forever. You will neither be able to leave the castle grounds nor reveal your past."

Sheriff Hurst began pulling Edlyn toward the marble platform. In a daze, Edlyn stumbled to keep up. She saw nothing and felt nothing, and she no longer heard Maddock and Peyton's fierce protests. But as the sheriff positioned her at the base of the platform, Edlyn finally started regaining her senses. A tiny spark of fight caught fire again within her, which gave her the courage to stare up at Raelin and Guthrie to make one final demand:

"Do what you will with me but release my friends first."

"Release them?" Guthrie laughed. "Of course we will not release them. Once the ceremony is complete, we will have the enjoyment of killing them while you watch."

"You promised," Edlyn seethed. "You made a vow."

Raelin's eyes sparkled maliciously. "I do not recall making any promise."

"Then you lied! The oath means nothing!" Edlyn proclaimed, grappling to free herself from the sheriff's hold.

Sheriff Hurst took Edlyn by the hair and threw his other arm around her neck, spinning her around so that she faced the cages. "Have a last look at your friends," he said cruelly in her ear.

"A very good idea," Raelin noted. "In fact, I shall bring the girl's companions closer so they can witness the binding ceremony before they die."

Raelin pointed to Peyton's cage. Its door flung open. Raelin waved her hand again, and Peyton began to be dragged forward. Though he attempted mightily to get away from the power that controlled him, he was steadily pulled closer. Once at the base of the podium, Peyton was thrown to the floor and somehow held down, barely able to move.

Next, Raelin motioned to Maddock's cage, and its door also swung aside. Maddock fought and resisted, but his efforts were no match for the power that soon tossed him down beside Peyton and prevented him from getting away.

Finally, Raelin swept her hand toward the cage at the back of the hall. The door to Ronan's cage opened.

"I allowed you to imprison me, but you will not be able to harm me, Raelin," Ronan spoke up calmly. "Nor you, Guthrie."

Raelin stopped. "What did you say?"

"How do you know our identities?" Guthrie barked, squinting to see Ronan in the torchlight.

"He knew my true name, too," Sheriff Hurst announced nervously, wrestling to keep Edlyn in his grip. "He said that he is from the Colleland."

Ronan stepped out of the cage under his own power and started walking closer. "Enough of this. Let them go."

"How dare you address me this way," Raelin fumed, raising her arms to unleash her terrible power once more.

Ronan emerged into the light. "I said let them go."

Raelin's eyes grew wide. "This cannot be," she whispered.

"Tiernan?" Guthrie asked, his voice shaking as he stared at him. "Is it you?"

"Yes, my brother and sister." Ronan looked between them. "It is I. Our paths cross again at long last."

Guthrie gasped.

"You lie," Raelin accused, though she was becoming even more pale. "Tiernan is dead."

Ronan shook his head. "You are mistaken. I live on, just as you do."

Kept down on the floor by the indiscernible power, Maddock managed only to raise his head. "Ronan? What are you talking about? What is going on?"

Ronan's expression softened as he looked meaningfully down at Maddock. Maddock gazed back at him, a glimmer of stunned realization appearing in his eyes.

Guthrie watched the silent exchange and turned nervously to his sister. "Could it really be? Could Tiernan still be alive?"

Seeming to collect herself, Raelin sneered. "Of course not. They are all lying. Only I have the power to create a blood spell. This man is an imposter." She finished by pointing her hands contemptuously at Ronan once again.

"Do not harm me, Raelin," Ronan cautioned, looking at her squarely. "Not if you value your own life."

Raelin hesitated. Her face contorted, and her nostrils flared angrily. With an angry sound, she slowly dropped her arms back to her sides.

"You had better explain yourself," Guthrie told Ronan in a low voice. "Or I shall kill you myself."

Ronan took another step nearer to the platform. "Not long after I was forced to flee to the Colleland all those centuries ago, I was involved in a serious hunting accident. I should have died, but somehow I survived. In the years that followed, I discovered that my body not only healed from human ailments with unusual ease and speed, but it had stopped aging altogether. I realized that some sort of magic must have changed me, and I knew that only a blood spell could wield such power. I also knew that it had to be a blood spell you created, Raelin, undoubtedly to allow you and Guthrie to live forever."

Guthrie peered suspiciously at Ronan. "But the blood spell was only put on Raelin and me, not on Tiernan."

Ronan shook his head. "So you thought. However, there was one crucial thing you both overlooked. By casting a blood spell upon yourselves as siblings, it meant that I, too, your blood brother, would be affected by the same magic. I, too, would live forever."

Guthrie glanced at Raelin, apprehensive. "Is he right? Is that possible?"

There was a terrible silence.

"Yes, it is possible," the queen eventually replied in a loathing, fearsome tone. "It was a significant oversight, indeed."

Ronan went on, "And as you must know, a blood spell meant that my blood descendents would also inherit some of that magic. While they would not inherit enough to live forever, the blood spell would bind them to me and, therefore, to you."

As Raelin listened, her breathing became strained and her expression was livid.

"It was a curse that I would gladly have relinquished, had I been able," Ronan continued thoughtfully. "To watch family and friends age and die, to live on while everyone I loved had left this life...there was nothing about the prospect of a never-ending mortal life that brought me joy."

As he spoke, Ronan took yet another step forward. He put his eyes on Edlyn, who remained trapped in the sheriff's arms. Edlyn realized that Ronan had positioned himself next to her sword, which was still on the ground. Edlyn nodded discretely, letting him know that she had understood. Ronan refocused on the king and queen and kept talking:

"But I realized that I could turn my curse into a blessing for the people of Nereth. I staged my death. I assumed a new identity. In disguise, I returned regularly to Nereth, for your curse could not keep me away from the land that was rightfully mine. I have been walking among the people of Nereth and the Colleland, known in this kingdom as the Man in White, ever since."

Raelin staggered. "It really is you, Tiernan."

His eyes shone. "Yes. I am Tiernan. I am the one they call the Man in White. I have been watching and preparing. I have taught those who remained loyal. I have been waiting for the day when our paths would cross again."

Holding Edlyn in his vice-like grip, Sheriff Hurst made an astonished sound and swayed slightly.

Raelin unexpectedly threw her head back and cackled. "You do not frighten me, Tiernan. It does not matter who you are. Even the blood spell cannot protect you from more of my own magic."

Again Raelin pointed at Tiernan, about to strike. Edlyn quickly rammed her elbows into the unsuspecting Sheriff Hurst and pushed him into the queen, causing both the sheriff and Raelin to fall to the floor.

Maddock made a shout. The queen's power disrupted, he and Peyton were able to spring to their feet and ready their weapons. Tiernan grabbed the sword that was on the ground and went to Edlyn's side.

"Enough!" Raelin screeched, pulling herself to her knees.

At a crazed motion of the queen's hands, a blast of wind swept through the hall, throwing Peyton, Maddock, Edlyn, and Tiernan back to the floor. Edlyn attempted to get up despite the heavy weight that seemed to be upon her, but she could not. Turning her head, she saw that the others were also held down by a power they could not see.

"Edlyn," Maddock panted, "are you alright?"

"I am alright," she told him, putting her eyes on his.

Storming back to the podium, Raelin vehemently made a different gesture with her arm. A golden altar appeared before her. "Grab the girl, Sheriff Hurst," she hissed.

Edlyn saw a frenzied look in the sheriff's eyes as he tugged her up beside him.

"Come forward, girl," Raelin ordered.

Edlyn did not obey. Outraged, Raelin pointed at her, and Edlyn felt her entire body go limp. Sweaty and shaking, the sheriff caught Edlyn and carried her to the altar, setting her upon it. Unable to move, Edlyn was terrified to feel her hands and legs become tied down by icy cords.

"Now kneel," Raelin instructed Sheriff Hurst.

Trembling and pasty white, the sheriff knelt at the altar beside Edlyn.

Raelin leaned over Edlyn, scowling with hatred. "Once this binding ceremony is performed, you will be trapped here and unable to tell anyone what you know.

You will be alone with your memories and your secrets, left to live the rest of your life with the sheriff."

"Raelin," Tiernan called, "take me as a prisoner, instead."

Raelin lifted her eyes, appearing amused. "Why should I choose between you, brother? I intend to destroy you both. I do not need to make a bargain."

"You should bargain," Tiernan insisted steadily. "For if you curse her, you shall also curse yourself."

Raelin smirked. "A noble attempt to save her, Tiernan, but I am not fooled. This girl has no power over my magic."

"Raelin, you are wrong," Tiernan said, his voice becoming deep and resolute.

Raelin's smirk disappeared. "Why should I believe you, Tiernan? Why should I believe that her fate would affect mine?"

"Because, as her necklace proves, Edlyn is my last remaining descendent. Bound to me, and to you, if you kill her, the blood spell that is upon all of us will be broken forever."

16

Edlyn's mind was racing.

Jaw clenched, Raelin used her cold hand to pull back the collar of Edlyn's dress, revealing the silver chain around her neck and the emblem hanging from it.

"You stole this, girl," Raelin whispered, livid.

"The necklace is rightfully hers," Tiernan pronounced. "It previously belonged to her mother, who was born in the Colleland."

"It cannot be!" Raelin exclaimed.

"It is just as I say," Tiernan asserted. "Edlyn's mother was the only child of my last remaining descendent. That is why, when her Edlyn's mother was yet still an infant, I put the emblem upon her. Years later, after her mother died in childbirth, ownership of the necklace rightfully passed to Edlyn."

Edlyn's heart was beating faster and faster with everything Tiernan was saying. Though overwhelmed by his declarations, somehow she knew that they were true.

Tiernan continued, his words penetrating the silence, "You know the magic, Raelin. You know there is a weakness in a blood spell: that those under a blood spell depend on one another for survival. What happens to one affects another. If someone harms or kills another who is under the same blood spell, the magic is weakened. And if it is the last descendent who is killed, the blood spell is broken forever. So if you harm Edlyn, you will profoundly harm yourselves."

Raelin screamed furiously.

Guthrie began to pace. "Over the centuries, our spies in the Colleland have eliminated countless numbers of your descendents, Tiernan. Raelin and I suffered no harm, so why should killing this girl—this last descendent of yours—be any different?"

"Yes, you have killed a great many innocent people," Tiernan agreed mournfully. "What you did not realize was that, with every one of my descendents you murdered, you were weakening the blood spell. You were slightly and gradually hurting yourselves."

Guthrie stopped in his tracks. "That is a lie!"

"No, it is the truth," Tiernan responded, powerfully resolute.

Raelin's face blanched, and she turned to Guthrie. "Then we must bind the girl to stay within the castle, as we originally planned. It is the only solution."

"Remember, whatever you do to Edlyn will affect you as well," Tiernan advised, almost patiently. "If you bind Edlyn, you also will be trapped here forever."

Raelin made a crazed sound and pointed her arms at Tiernan. He suddenly let out a yell of immense pain. At that same moment, a terrible sensation struck Edlyn's body, causing her to scream. As Edlyn's cry died away, she could hear Raelin and Guthrie also screaming in agony.

"Stop, Raelin! Do not strike Tiernan again!" Guthrie was grasping his chest. "You injure us as well!"

"Peyton, get up!" Maddock shouted, getting to his feet. "Raelin's power has been weakened!"

Edlyn realized that she could move again, and she felt the cords that had tied her down disappear. Panting from the pain coursing through her, Edlyn rolled off the altar. Raelin, wincing with pain, pointed hatefully at her, ready to strike.

"Raelin, do not harm the girl!" Guthrie yelled. "You will hurt us even more!"

Raelin stopped. Her eyes moved from Edlyn to Tiernan, who remained on the floor. Tipping her head, she next observed Peyton and Maddock, who stood with weapons ready as if ready to pounce. Slowly, a cunning smile appeared on Raelin's face.

"Do not worry, Guthrie. We are in no danger," she assured her brother. "Tiernan cannot harm us, since he would also be harming himself, and his pathetic friends will not attack, for they know that doing so would greatly weaken Tiernan and the girl."

Crouched behind the altar, Edlyn saw Maddock and Peyton exchange glances and hesitantly lower their weapons.

"So we are at a draw." Guthrie uneasily put his own sword away.

Raelin shook her head. "No, Guthrie, we still have the advantage. These pitiful boys will not hurt us, but we can kill them without significant consequence."

"Wait, Your Highness," Sheriff Hurst uttered, coming forward. Sweating, tremulous, and wild-eyed, he spoke in a strange low tone, "Do not kill these young men yet, for I want them to suffer first. If I cannot have Edlyn, no one shall."

With a wild cry, Sheriff Hurst lunged for Edlyn, his sword poised to kill her. Edlyn frantically moved to get out of the way but slipped on the slick marble and fell backward.

"Stop, Sheriff Hurst!" Raelin's commanded.

The sheriff did not obey. Edlyn let out a scream. But just before the sheriff reached her, he suddenly halted and made a peculiar sound, his eyes shocked and hollow with surprise. Edlyn then saw that Maddock's dagger was lodged in the sheriff's chest. She turned and saw Maddock breathing fast, his arm still extended out in the sheriff's direction.

Sheriff Hurst took one final step toward Edlyn before putting his fading sight on Peyton. "Your father was my adoptive older brother," Sheriff Hurst managed to say, blood oozing from his wound. He dropped to one knee and turned his head to Maddock. "I was the one who killed your parents."

Sheriff Hurst said no more. He let fell forward and let out his last breath.

The young men stared at the sheriff's corpse in stunned silence. Taking advantage of their distraction, Guthrie sprinted for Maddock and Peyton, ready to kill. Peyton did a double take and reached for his axe.

"Do not to harm Guthrie!" Maddock told Peyton. "It will weaken Ronan and Edlyn!"

Guthrie swung his sword to strike Peyton, who only used his axe to block the blow. Maddock dove in, trying to pry the weapon from Guthrie's hands. Edlyn scrambled to her feet, retrieving the dead sheriff's sword and Maddock's dagger. Just as she was about to join the fight, she heard Raelin let out a chilling yell. Edlyn raised her eyes. The queen was pointing her hands directly at Maddock.

"Maddock! Look out!" Edlyn shouted, but she knew it was too late.

Maddock turned, but all he could do was flinch in anticipation of the deadly impact. For Edlyn, what happened next seemed to occur slow-motion: Tiernan got up and leapt in front of Maddock, let out a new scream of agony, and collapsed once more. Guthrie, still under Maddock's hold, became unnaturally still. Then Raelin herself, with an awful cry, crumpled onto the thrones.

"You...you have sacrificed yourself, Tiernan," Raelin told him faintly. "You have sacrificed...us all."

Her eyes closed, and she rolled onto the marble platform below.

"Ronan!"

Maddock's cry of despair resonated through the great hall. He rushed to Tiernan, who remained motionless on the floor.

"Ronan!" Maddock cried again. "Can you hear me? Ronan!"

Edlyn got to her knees and attempted to crawl to Maddock, but the excruciating pain in her body was too much. With a moan, Edlyn set herself onto her stomach, certain that she was going to die.

"Edlyn?" Peyton sped toward her. "Edlyn, what is wrong?"

Maddock whipped his head up, his face becoming white when he saw that Edlyn was hurt.

Edlyn pushed herself onto her hands. "I...I am alright," she lied.

Tiernan stirred.

"He is alive!" Maddock exclaimed, carefully resting Tiernan's head in his hands.

A sound like a thunderclap filled the hall. Edlyn glanced back and saw that a massive crack had appeared down the middle of the marble platform, causing the thrones to topple over. A moment later, the floor of the great hall began rumbling, and everything started to violently shake.

"This whole place is going to come down!" Peyton shouted as a pillar collapsed and shattered.

"We need to get out of here!" Maddock slung Tiernan's arm over his shoulder.

"Leave me, Maddock," Tiernan muttered, unable to even support his own head. "I am done for."

"No." Maddock determinedly hoisted Tiernan to his feet. "I am not leaving you."

While the quaking intensified, Peyton helped Edlyn to her feet and then ran to assist Maddock with carrying Tiernan. Her pain fading, Edlyn hurried to join them. Together, the group charged for the doors as fast as they could go. Stones smashed down. Cracks began appearing in the walls and ceiling. Torches fell.

"When you reach the foyer, go left...to the back of the castle...to the river," Tiernan directed them, his voice barely audible.

Archways fell. The floor shifted and sank. Just as the entire hall started to collapse, the group reached the foyer. A huge chandelier fell in front of them, spraying shards of glass everywhere.

"This way!" Maddock shouted over the din, pointing left.

Tiernan attempted to lift his head, made an incoherent noise, and fell silent. Maddock, Peyton, and Edlyn carried him, dodging the falling wreckage. Up ahead, they saw light from a doorway.

"We are almost there!" Peyton shouted.

The group raced outside. Blinking to adjust to the sunlight, Edlyn could see a grassy hill that sloped down to the edge of the river.

"Keep moving!" Maddock bellowed.

The three of them sprinted onward with their wounded companion, fleeing downhill to the riverbank. Once they were at the water's edge, they turned around and looked back. The massive castle was starting to sway.

"Get down!" Peyton ordered.

Edlyn dropped and tucked her head, and Peyton crouched protectively over her. Maddock hurled himself on top of Tiernan. The massive noise of the castle's collapse rang in Edlyn's ears as the earth rocked.

Then, suddenly, all was calm.

Edlyn slowly lifted her head. She gasped at the sight that met her eyes. The castle was gone, replaced by heaps of stone and rubble. The empty castle courtyard was in the distance.

Tiernan made another groan.

"Ronan," Maddock said, carefully laying him flat.

Tiernan gazed up at him. "Maddock, my time has come."

"Do not say that." Maddock looked to Edlyn and Peyton, desperation in his eyes. "What can we do?"

Edlyn crawled to Maddock's side. "I can try to make a healing potion."

"Tell me what you need," Peyton said to her.

Edlyn hurriedly scanned the foliage near them. "I need herbs. I need—"

"It is of no use, friends," Tiernan interrupted tranquilly. "This is something that no potion can heal. Raelin's strike was meant to kill."

"We are not going to let you die," Maddock contended.

Tiernan smiled. "You are not letting me die. It is my time."

"No," Maddock whispered.

"I will be glad to pass on," Tiernan told them, watching the sky. "No one should live as a mortal forever. We are supposed to go on to our next adventure."

As gentle breeze stirred the trees, a motion caught Edlyn's attention. She looked up. Through her tears, she saw Ailith and Kegan standing nearby.

"The great Tiernan," Kegan said respectfully. With his green eyes shimmering brightly in the sunlight, he came to Tiernan's side and dropped to one knee.

Ailith followed and bowed her head. "We remain loyal to you, Tiernan, as the rightful heir to the throne of Nereth."

"You have been valiant friends," Tiernan told them. "The Kingdom of Nereth shall never forget what you have done."

"You Langerlen do not fear to leave the forest now," Peyton observed.

Ailith smiled a little. "The power of Guthrie and Raelin has been weakened significantly."

"Weakened?" Peyton repeated. "But surely they are dead. Blood spell or not, the castle collapsed upon them. They could not have survived. How can their power remain at all?"

Tiernan managed to motion toward the rubble where the castle had stood. "Do not be afraid. If they survived, they are of no danger to you now."

"Then what about Edlyn?" Maddock asked apprehensively. "She has been weakened, too, has she not?"

"She will recover," Tiernan replied, smiling at Edlyn. "She has her father's blood in her, which was not bound by the same spell. Her body will heal."

Edlyn took Tiernan by the hand. "My father told me about the day he met you. You came to him after my mother died, and it was an immense comfort to him."

Tiernan's eyes glistened. "Edlyn, you have grown into a resilient, smart young woman, just as I knew you would. I am glad for this chance to speak with you before I die. You see, when your mother was born, I knew that she was the only child born to my last remaining descendant. Fearing that your mother's heritage would be discovered by Raelin and Guthrie's murderous spies, I did not have your mother marked on her shoulder in the usual way. And when she was still an infant, I hid her in the only place Raelin's spies would not think to look: Nereth itself."

A tear rolled down Edlyn's cheek. She held Tiernan's hand more closely as he continued:

"On a cold night a few days after your mother was born, I brought your mother and her parents to Nereth to start a new life. Your mother grew up as any other child in the kingdom. Her parents—your grandparents—faithfully never disclosed to your mother or anyone else what they knew. Your mother grew up hidden in plain sight."

Edlyn breathed in deeply. "You saved her from Raelin and Guthrie. Thank you, Tiernan."

"Yet I regret that your mother never knew of her true origins," he replied sadly. "I thought I was protecting her by keeping her in ignorance, but after her death, I wondered if I had done the right thing. It had been your mother's truth to know. That was why I went to your father. I explained to him what perhaps I should have told your mother long before."

"Do not apologize," Edlyn told him, crying softly. "You did what you thought was best."

"I did all that I could, yet it was not enough. Although she was my direct descendant, she also had the blood of non-descendents within her. Your mother succumbed to the natural travails of childbirth like so many others."

Edlyn put her hand on the chain that hung from her neck. "My father told me to always protect this. I never realized what it meant."

"It was intended as a way to mark the last remaining descendant," Tiernan stated. "I placed the emblem on a tiny chain and put it upon your mother after she was born. She wore it throughout her life. After her death, I explained to your father its true meaning, and I instructed him to keep the emblem for you."

Edlyn gently released Tiernan's hand, using her own to wipe the tears from her face. Tiernan watched her for a last, long moment and then turned his head to Peyton.

"You are Peyton."

Peyton nodded. "Yes, sir."

"It has been an honor to fight alongside you, Peyton."

"Thank you," Peyton replied, his voice not quite steady. "My father told me much of you before he died."

"Your father was a good man," Tiernan replied.

Peyton blinked hard. "Yes, he was."

Tiernan looked again at Maddock. "When your parents were killed by Sheriff Hurst, I knew that I needed to take you into my care."

"You have been like a father to me, Ronan," Maddock told him. I meant to repay you for all that you did, but instead, I am watching you die. I shall never forgive myself."

"Maddock, listen to me," Tiernan's voice regained some strength. "You have been brave and true. You have been everything a father could wish for. I am as proud of you as I know your real father would have been."

Maddock breathed in slowly.

Tiernan went on, "When I first met you in the village, you were only a small boy, but I sensed that you were destined for great things. After your parents were killed, I realized that I had to teach you all I knew before fate called you on your journey, which was certain to be significant."

Maddock let his tears fall freely. "I am sorry that I could not save you."

"It was I who needed to save you, Maddock. I am sure there is still more to the journey you are meant to fulfill. That is why I let myself get captured on that night we fought Sheriff Hurst and why I let myself get struck by Raelin. I sacrificed myself so you could be free."

Tiernan broke off and looked up at the sky. The songs of the birds and the gentle sound of the river drifted through the air. A few moments passed, and then Tiernan looked upon them again.

"Farewell, my friends."

Tiernan's eyes closed. He was gone.

Epilogue

Edlyn stood alone on the stage, looking over the seemingly endless crowd that filled the grassy field before her. Behind the crowd were remnants of the fallen castle and the foundation of the building being raised in its place. The sun was just starting to set, its golden light touching the trees of Ravenshire Forest. Edlyn took a deep breath. The time had come.

"Who will join the Council of Nereth to represent Ravenshire Forest to the west?" Edlyn asked in a loud, firm voice.

"We will."

The response had come from Ailith, who came out of the audience, followed by Kegan. Several more Langerlen watched happily from nearby.

"We come in peace," Kegan added, giving Edlyn a bow.

Edlyn curtsied, and then she spoke to the crowd again, "Who will join the Council of Nereth to represent the hills to the east?"

"I will."

Peyton stepped forward, with Vanora and other farmers of their lands close behind him.

"I come in peace," Peyton finished ceremonially with a slight nod.

Edlyn watched him for a moment, and then she went on, "Who will join the Council of Nereth to represent the Colleland to the North?"

"I will." Maddock emerged from the center of the audience, where the citizens of the Colleland were gathered. "I come in peace."

Edlyn was almost certain that Maddock winked at her. She smiled slightly before continuing:

"And I will represent the land of Nereth," she announced, peeking at Lancy, who smiled proudly from the front of the crowd. "I, too, come in peace. The Council of Nereth is completed, and the land is unified once again."

The audience burst into cheers and applause. Hugs and tears were shared. Strangers shook hands. Children sang. When the crowd finally quieted down, Edlyn spoke again:

"Today, we have a chance to start anew. This land has been released from the oppressive hold of Raelin and Guthrie. So, in the name of Tiernan and the people of this land, I bring forth the newly elected head of the Council of Nereth."

While cheering again, the masses parted, making a way for Briac to step onto the stage. He held up his trembling hands, and the people gradually hushed.

"Dear friends," Briac began, "I stand before you as one who is very humbled. I am only here because of the brave, faithful efforts of so many others. Let us remember what we have lived through and use those memories to become something better. Let us never forget the wisdom of King Whittemoor or Tiernan."

"Hear! Hear!" someone shouted.

Another man raised his hand triumphantly. "Hear! Hear!"

While the crowd broke into celebration once again, Edlyn stepped back and slipped down from the stage. Easily disappearing among the throng, Edlyn wove a path to the edge of the audience and walked off by herself. Strolling over the grass while the evening birds sang, Edlyn rolled back the sleeves of her dress and pulled her loose hair into a braid. The sun had nearly set by the time she reached the river. She watched the water for a while and then closed her eyes, letting the wind pass soothingly over her face.

A horse's familiar whinny reached her ears.

"Cynric!" Edlyn exclaimed, spinning around.

Kegan was leading her horse toward her. Beside him, Ailith was guiding Zanavian. Edlyn ran up and threw her arms around the horses' necks. Zanavian snorted playfully. Cynric gave her a nudge.

"They have been missing you," Ailith remarked. She motioned to Cynric. "Especially this one."

Edlyn quickly wiped a tear from her face and gave Cynric another hug. "I admit that I have missed them, too."

"Now that you have your horses, I suppose that you will no longer need to sneak rides in the back of my wagon," someone commented.

Edlyn laughed and turned around. Peyton was striding across the grass, leading one of his own horses by the reins.

Edlyn shrugged. "You never know, Peyton. As we are now members of the Council of Nereth, there may be another journey in store for us yet."

Peyton eyed her. "I do not doubt it."

Only once Peyton stopped in front of her did Edlyn realize that the Langerlen were gone. Edlyn peered up at Peyton, a lump forming in her throat.

"Peyton, I know that no words could ever convey the thanks that you and your mother deserve. But I will always be grateful. We would have died, had it not been for you."

Peyton replied simply, "You are welcome, Edlyn."

In a swell of emotion, Edlyn threw her arms around him. Peyton made a muffled, surprised sound in response. After a few moments, Edlyn let go and stepped back. Peyton was staring at her, his mouth slightly open and his cheeks a light shade of pink.

Zanavian started to whinny excitedly, causing Edlyn to look behind her. Maddock was approaching.

"I am sorry," Maddock said uncertainly, looking between Edlyn and Peyton. "I did not mean to—"

"You had better come greet Zanavian," Edlyn told him with a laugh, trying to keep the horse from bolting. "She is quite anxious to see you."

Maddock resumed coming forward. Zanavian tugged until she broke free from Edlyn's grip and ran to meet him.

"Easy, girl. It is good to see you, too," Maddock said in the horse's ear, leading her back to join the others.

Peyton cleared his throat. "I should go find my mother," he told them with a nod and began walking away with his horse.

"Peyton," Maddock called after him.

Peyton stopped and looked back.

"Thank you, friend," Maddock said.

Peyton smiled. "It was a privilege, Maddock."

Without saying more, Peyton went to rejoin the crowd. Another gentle gust of wind blew as Edlyn looked over at Maddock.

He gestured to his new clothes. "So, Edlyn, am I cleaned up enough for you now?"

Edlyn tipped her head, observing him. "You know, I think I like the old Maddock better."

"Good." He pulled off his cape and ran a hand messily through his hair. "I do, too."

Edlyn smiled.

Maddock grinned in return, but his expression soon became thoughtful. "Edlyn, about all that happened and all that you had to endure...I am sorry."

"Maddock, do not be sorry. As I told you before, I—"

"I know, but I am sorry, nonetheless. I am sorry for what you had to go through, and I am sorry for some of the things that I said and did." He breathed in deeply. "It is good that you are as stubborn as I am, Edlyn, for the truth was, as much as I did not want to admit it, I needed you."

Edlyn's chest warmed and tears filled her eyes. "Well, I think that I...I needed you, too, Maddock."

He looked out at the river. "Edlyn, we cannot say what is in store for us or for Nereth. Nothing is certain. We do not even know if enemies remain. There will still be much to do as members of the council." He paused, as if trying to find the right words. "Edlyn, if things were different..."

Edlyn caught her breath. "What, Maddock?"

He reached out and took her by the hand. "We should be getting back."

Edlyn nodded. "Yes, Maddock. There is much we must do."

As the sun finished setting, Edlyn and Maddock took their horses by the reins and walked back to the crowd, side by side.

ABOUT THE AUTHOR

TJ Amberson hails from Seattle, Washington. When not writing, she can likely be found spending time with her husband, working as an emergency room physician, traveling, attempting to garden, playing the piano, or drinking hot chocolate. TJ strives to provide original, age-appropriate, and well-written novels for tweens, teens, and new adults.

BOOKS BY TJ AMBERSON

(*Available or coming in 2017*)
THE KINGDOM OF NERETH
CHANGED MATTER
BETWEEN
WHITE COATS AND STETHOSCOPES

www.tjamberson.com
She can also be followed on Facebook

Made in the USA
San Bernardino, CA
15 March 2017